OUR OWN LITTLE
PARADISE

MARIANNE KAURIN

OUR OWN LITTLE
PARADISE

Translated from the Norwegian by Olivia Lasky

Arctis

This translation has been published with the financial support of NORLA, Norwegian Literature Abroad.

W1-Media, Inc.
Arctis Books USA
Stamford, CT, USA

Copyright © 2022 by W1-Media Inc. for this edition
Text copyright © Marianne Kaurin
Syden first published by H. Aschehoug & Co. (W. Nygaard) AS, 2018
Published in agreement with Oslo Literary Agency
First hardcover English edition published by
W1-Media Inc. / Arctis USA 2022

Visit our website at www.arctis-books.com
1 3 5 7 9 8 6 4 2
The Library of Congress Control Number: 2021944680
ISBN 978-1-64690-018-3
eBook ISBN 978-1-64690-618-5

English translation copyright © Olivia Lasky, 2022
Jacket art and hand lettering by Friederike Ablang

Printed in Germany, European Union

Today's the last day. Just a few hours left. Then it's over.

This isn't the kind of ending you need to cry about. There's no ax murderer or meteorite or plague. This is a good ending. Most people have been looking forward to it, counting down the weeks on the calendar, packing bags, and buying flip-flops. I've been telling people that I'm excited. It'll be *so* nice, I say, as I calculate how much time we're talking about.

I've always liked counting things. Days and minutes. Hair ties, pens, friends. It kind of just happens automatically. I have fourteen purple pencils in my pencil case, even though my favorite color is blue. There are forty-eight steps from the third floor down to the backyard and forty-two steps over to the ugly sign that welcomes you to Chaplin Court. I've already been alive for over four thousand days. I've lived in six apartments, in three towns. I've been in six different grades. I've had three friends with names that start with the letter *m*.

I don't talk to any of them now, but *m* is my favorite letter.

If someone asked me how many steps there are between the gym and the classroom, I'd be able to give them the answer. And now I'm standing right here, right outside the gym, on my way to the classroom. The asphalt is sizzling, and the flag is flying. Olivia and Emma are leaning against the fence bordering the high school like they can't wait to get started there. They're standing in the group everyone wants to be in—they *are* the group. All of them have tight tops and long hair. Emma is holding up her phone, trying to get the whole gang into a picture as they giggle.

I walk past them with my mouth shut. It's best to count in your head, I think, and see Olivia making a duck-face into the camera before turning back to the others.

Marcus is standing with a group of boys by the flagpole. He's wearing a red T-shirt and his face and arms are already tan. I can hear his laughter all the way over here, even though I'm more than sixty steps away from that wonderful sound. I really should count out loud when I'm walking past him just so he *might* notice that I actually exist, but then I'd be the weird girl, and it's already enough to be the new one.

Joanna and some of the other girls from class are standing by the entrance, staring longingly at the swings.

Joanna is wearing a windbreaker even though it's about a hundred degrees out, and she still has her bike helmet on. They're talking about a Girl Scout camp they're going to after their family vacations. It's going to be tons of fun, I hear them say. I might have been able to join this group. Maybe I could have even gone to camp as well. But all I can think about is over by the flagpole and the middle school, where there are people who could *really* lift me up.

So I do as I always do: I just say hi and speed toward the entrance, up the stairs to the second floor, and into the classroom with the windows facing the playground. The classroom that's always quiet, like it's waiting for something.

I've just settled in by the window to get a good view of a certain flagpole when the door swings open. A headful of curls pops in—a boy.

"Hi."

He stands in the doorway, staring at me, only his head in view. I've never seen him before, so I just stand there. He smiles. His eyes are big.

"This is 6A, right?"

He takes a step backward into the hallway, closes the door, and then opens it again. He was probably checking the schedule hanging outside. I nod and hurry away from the window. I sit down at my desk and pretend I'm doing something important as I root around in my pencil case.

"What's your name?" he asks, stepping into the classroom.

He looks around and smiles, like he's never been in a classroom before, like *this* classroom is so different and so much nicer than any other ordinary classroom. He has one hand in his pocket and is holding a hat in the other. His T-shirt is from the zoo, and his poop-brown shorts look way too big, sagging in the most uncool way possible. He's going sockless in some canvas sneakers that were probably white about a hundred years ago. His arms and legs are thin and pale and his curls bounce up and down on his head, even when he's standing still.

"Nora," I reply.

"Got it," he says, smiling even wider. One of his front teeth is crooked.

"I'm Wilmer."

He doesn't say anything else—just looks at me like he's waiting for me to get the conversation going. Like it's *my* responsibility somehow. I could've asked where he's from and what he's doing in our classroom, or whether he likes going to the zoo or about the shorts that are way too big for him, but I don't have time because now the bell is ringing and after four seconds the level of noise in the classroom is sky-high. The boy named Wilmer leans against the wall in the very back. It doesn't seem like anyone even notices him. They're all just laughing and talking and messing around. Because it's the last day of school—a half-day. Soon it will be over. Three hours with our teacher, Ms. Gustavsen, and then summer break can start.

There are fifty-four days in summer break. I counted on the calendar hanging on the fridge. Fifty-four days is the same as one thousand two hundred and ninety-six hours. Which is seventy-seven thousand seven hundred and sixty minutes. I haven't calculated the seconds yet, but it's probably a lot. Millions, even.

Now Ms. Gustavsen is standing in front of us on the very last day of sixth grade. She's wearing a light-yellow dress for the occasion and quite a bit of makeup. Her lips are a shimmery pink and her hair is gathered in a mushroomy bun on top of her head.

"Welcome, my dears, to the last day of sixth grade," she says ceremoniously, looking out over the classroom like a queen addressing her subjects.

She takes off her round glasses and puts one end in her mouth, something she does about every other minute. And since she's always sucking on her glasses and wears so much lipstick, she often has pink behind her ears. There are a lot of people in the class who think Ms. Gustavsen is lame. They mock her waddling walk and make fun of her weird clothes. It seems like Ms. Gustavsen doesn't care, though. Once she caught Marcus imitating her, waddling around the classroom and cackling like a hen while she watched from the door. Marcus was super embarrassed, but Ms. Gustavsen just laughed.

"You're a bit of a chicken yourself!" she said as she headed out for yard duty in the neon safety vest that sits a little too snugly on her saggy breasts.

Now she's pointing toward the wall at the back of the classroom, and everyone turns around. Whispering spreads throughout the room as people spot the unfamiliar boy in the silly clothes. People in this class are *very* particular about clothes.

"There you are!" Ms. Gustavsen says to the boy who calls himself Wilmer. "It's so nice you had the chance to come by."

She goes to the back of the classroom and greets him, pulling him over to the chalkboard at the front of the room.

"We have a visitor!" she announces, grasping his shoulders and the T-shirt from the zoo.

She looks proud, like she's introducing a newborn baby to her family for the first time.

"And this boy, ladies and gentlemen, will be starting in our class this fall. Today he's just here to say hi."

She leans down toward Wilmer.

"You can tell everyone your name," she continues.

"Wilmer," he says with a loud, clear voice.

Someone snickers.

"Precisely," says Ms. Gustavsen. "Wilmer just moved here. Where is it that you live again?"

"Thirty Miller Avenue," Wilmer says. "Building F."

He sounds like a little boy who just learned to recite his own address.

"Precisely," Ms. Gustavsen says again. "That's Chaplin Court, isn't it?"

Now there are even more people who snicker. I don't know what's so funny about Chaplin Court, apart from the fact that its nickname is Craplin and that it would definitely win first prize if there were a contest for the ugliest place you could possibly live.

"Nora lives in Chaplin Court, too," Ms. Gustavsen says, pointing at me. "So you can walk to school together after summer break."

I actually do like Ms. Gustavsen, but right now she's really starting to annoy me. Why does she get to decide that I'm going to hang out with a guy with big shorts and zoo T-shirts just because he lives in Chaplin Court, too? Why does she have to talk about Chaplin Court at all? It's nice that Ms. Gustavsen is trying to help me make friends, though. She's been trying to do that ever since

I started here at the beginning of the year. But I need friends who bring me *up*, not down, and Wilmer seems like he's *definitely* the type to bring me down.

Wilmer is finally allowed to leave the front of the room and sit on a chair at the very back. He tries to meet my eyes when he walks past my desk as if we're already best friends. Just because we live close to each other and met ten seconds before everyone else came into the classroom. I quickly look the other way.

"Ms. Gustavsen!"

Olivia is waving an arm and starts talking.

"Can we go around the class so everyone can talk about what they're doing over the summer?" she asks.

It seems like a lot of people think this is a great idea. Majorca, Mexico, and France are shouted out. Olivia has gotten halfway out of her chair and is waving her arms to try to organize what apparently so many people want to take part in. Ms. Gustavsen suggests that maybe not everyone needs to participate, but Olivia is so worked up she doesn't even hear her.

"Vanessa can start!" she shouts, pointing at the desk by the window in the first row.

One of my legs starts trembling and my mouth goes dry. Then Vanessa starts. She's going to southern Italy for three weeks. Olivia points to Theo so that everyone will understand that we're moving from front to back, desk by desk. I count to ten and put my hand on top of my leg so it won't tremble as much. Ten desks until it's my turn. Theo is going to Croatia. Sara is going to Spain for a few weeks. Simon, who sits behind Sara, is going to Florida. He speaks in a loud, clear voice, and several people sigh enviously. Alexandra, behind Simon, says she wishes *she* were the one traveling as far as Florida but she's only going to Denmark.

"But next year," Alexandra continues proudly, "we're going to Thailand for four weeks."

There are six left until it's my turn. Matt is going to Greece. Vera to Dubai. Everyone has plans for the summer, and everyone wants to tell the class all about them. *Everyone* is traveling. Abroad. People in this class are *very* concerned with traveling abroad. There was even a contest for who'd been to the most foreign countries. Emma won with twenty-seven.

I look at Ms. Gustavsen and then down at my desk as I hear that Olivia will be at a resort in Portugal for two weeks. I don't even really know what a resort is but it sounds nice. Soon it will be my turn. Soon I have to talk. My stomach is pounding, almost all the way up to my heart.

"My goodness," Ms. Gustavsen says. "So many of you are going out into the world! Do you know what I'll be doing?"

There are two people left before I have to talk, so it's fine with me that Ms. Gustavsen takes over for a bit while I can think some more about my own plans.

"I bought a little cabin! By a lake deep in the woods. My own little resort, you might call it. And I'll be spending the whole summer there, just reading and eating good food. That'll be nice, too, don't you think?"

No one responds, but a few people nod and some others grunt a little bit. As though Ms. Gustavsen's vacation plans stink. I mean, who wants to sit by a lake in the woods and read books?

Marcus is up next. He sits two desks ahead of me. I spend six hours every single day looking at his back. That's quite a lot of minutes if you add up a whole school year. I know his back by heart—I know exactly how it looks when he coughs or laughs, the small movements between his shoulder blades. I notice as soon as he gets a new sweater. I've probably spent two thousand hours imagining how it would be to let my hand glide from his neck down over the back I'm always staring at.

Marcus says that he's going to their cabin in the south of France first, and that they're leaving early tomorrow morning. Then he's spending a few weeks in Spain. He nods at Sara.

"But what I'm *most* excited about," he continues eagerly, "is going to London."

He looks around the classroom to make sure everyone is paying attention.

"Because then my dad and I are going to a Chelsea soccer match. And that'll be *crazy* cool, since he's as big a Chelsea fan as I am."

He smiles happily and turns around to face Julie. The skin on my face heats up like a kettle. Because I sit right behind Julie. So he's *almost* looking at me. There's just a few inches until his eyes meet mine.

Julie starts carefully, her voice a bit hoarse. Imagine if she doesn't have anything to tell, that not much is happening in fifty-four days, that she's just going to be at home. But of course that isn't the case. Nobody's just at *home* when it's summer.

Julie is going to Cyprus with her mom, and then she's going to France with her dad.

"That's what's so nice about having divorced parents," Julie says, happy as a clam. "You get *two* trips abroad, so it's like double the fun."

She turns in her seat and looks at me. Everyone is looking at me. Ms. Gustavsen, too. The classroom is silent. Completely silent. I know I need to open my mouth, that they're all wondering where I'm going this summer, what exciting plans I have with my family, what I'm going to do. I look from one to the other, at the expectant faces, but my mind is blank. There isn't a single word in there. I gape for a few seconds, clear my throat, and then a weak sound emerges from my vocal cords.

"This summer," I say, looking at Marcus.

He looks back at me. Now he's looking at *me*!

"This summer," I say once more, waiting to make up my mind.

"This summer, I'm going to the tropics."

Ms. Gustavsen nods encouragingly and smiles. Marcus is still looking at me. *Everyone* is looking at me. They want more.

"And I'm really excited about that," I say, imagining the pools and waterslides and the long white beaches, the parasols and the kids' club. Which I'm too big for, of course.

"I'm going to swim and sunbathe and relax. Just do . . . tropical things. For weeks. I'm leaving early tomorrow."

Suddenly I hear a snicker. Or to be precise, two. Olivia is leaning toward Emma, holding her hand over her mouth and whispering something.

"There's no *place* that's called the tropics," Emma says matter-of-factly.

She's vice president of the student council and is going to be a lawyer when she grows up, just like her mother.

"It just sounds so lame to say 'the tropics.'"

My leg is trembling again. Now my left arm, too. Can't we just move on now? Can't someone else take over?

"Where are you really going, Nora? 'The tropics' isn't a *country*."

They snicker again. Some others laugh, too. Luckily, Ms. Gustavsen takes over.

"It's quite common to say 'the tropics' even though it isn't a particular country on the map," she says. "It's what you call warm places where you can relax and swim and have fun in the sun. Just like Nora's going to do."

Ms. Gustavsen points at me in an irritating way, as though everyone in the class is senile and has suddenly forgotten who's going to the tropics.

"So the tropics can kind of be anywhere."

Ms. Gustavsen looks at Martina, who starts talking about her vacation plans. Luckily. Enough about the tropics. Martina is going to the mountains and on a bike tour. Patrick is going on a road trip for three weeks. Joanna is visiting her grandparents in northern Norway. Emma is going to the Canary Islands, which are in the tropics. She looks at me when she says "the tropics," pronouncing each syllable as if she were explaining it to a three-year-old or someone with brain damage.

"But before that, I'm going to Paris for a week to shop," she says proudly, looking at Olivia.

Ms. Gustavsen takes over when the rest of the class has talked about their summer plans.

"Then let's move on," she says, but then she catches sight of Wilmer in the back. "Ah, but we forgot to ask you, Wilmer! Do you have any exciting summer plans?"

Everyone turns to look at him. He smiles.

"I'm going to the tropics, too," he says, and looks at me.

What did he mean by that?

"Nah," he continues. "I'll be at home."

He looks at Ms. Gustavsen.

"My dad is broke, so there won't be any vacation this year."

He shrugs and looks out at the class. Of course there are a few snickers. There's *always* someone who snickers.

"No tropics for me," Wilmer says, smiling.

He says it as though it's totally fine that he isn't going anywhere. It looks like he's actually *excited* about summer break, even though he's just going to be at home. With his broke dad. In Craplin Court.

Now I've got an idea," Ms. Gustavsen says when the bell rings for last period.

She looks like a puppy who's about to be allowed to run free in the woods. Her yellow dress has sweat rings under each arm and her hair is plastered to her forehead.

"I read about something in a teachers' magazine that I thought sounded like so much fun! I want you all to get a pen, and I'll come around with a piece of paper for each of you."

She shuffles around the classroom, the scent of her strong perfume trailing behind her. A piece of paper lands on my desk. I stare at Marcus's back. He's sitting completely still with the piece of paper in his left hand.

"Now I want everyone to write their name at the top of the piece of paper you've just gotten," Ms. Gustavsen says, pointing at her paper. "And then I want you to write three sentences—three things you hope will happen over the summer."

She smiles contentedly and claps her hands together. "And you're allowed to dream a bit, too!" she laughs. "You can't just write things you *know* are going to happen. There's no point in that! Be a little crazy. Dare to dream. Then I want you to fold the paper, first once, and then once more."

She demonstrates with her own piece of paper. "Afterward I'll come around and gather all of the papers in this basket. They'll stay here at school all summer, and then you'll be able to read what you wrote when vacation is over and you start seventh grade. Doesn't that sound fun? Then you can see if any of it has actually happened!"

Everyone is sitting bent over their paper, writing. It's a difficult task. I shut my eyes since it's easier to think that way. What *do* I dream about happening? My mind is completely blank. There isn't even one single dream. I open my eyes again, and the first thing I see is Marcus's red T-shirt. Then I think of something. I smile as I write, putting my hand over the paper so no one can see. Ms. Gustavsen *did* say we were supposed to dream. And that's exactly what I'm doing... until someone taps me on the shoulder.

"Can I borrow a pen?"

It's the kid in the zoo T-shirt.

"I didn't bring anything with me," he says, smiling with

that crooked front tooth. I can't decide whether I think it's cute or ugly.

"I didn't think there was any point in bringing a pencil case or anything with me when I was just coming to visit."

I take a pencil out of my case and hand it to him. He smiles and looks down at what I wrote on the sheet. Then he smiles even more. I hurry to cover it up and Wilmer sits back down. I'd had a plan for the last two points, but now I've forgotten the whole thing. Just because of Wilmer, who just *had* to ask *me specifically* for a pen. I'm still thinking when Ms. Gustavsen says for the third time that everyone has to turn in their papers. I write down some nonsense that will never, *ever* happen, fold the sheet of paper, and hand it to Ms. Gustavsen. It gets mixed in with everyone else's dreams. Ms. Gustavsen hugs the basket against her chest like she's holding a kitten.

"I promise I won't peek," she says, laughing at herself.

She probably holds the world record for laughing at herself.

"And then we will see what's happened next year."

Ms. Gustavsen picks up the guitar and strikes a few chords. Several people in the class squirm in their seats, which is always what happens when the guitar shows up.

"Now we all get to sing my favorite Swedish ode to summer!" Ms. Gustavsen shouts, strumming eagerly.

Du skal inte tro det blir sooooommar,
i fall inte nån set- ter fart, på sommarn og gör
lite somrigt. Då kommer blommorna snart.

It's off-key and embarrassing, but it seems like Ms. Gustavsen can't get enough of it.

"Loooovely!" she shouts encouragingly, letting us make our way through all the verses. She's been having us practice singing this song since Easter. I bet she's been waiting for this "perfect" moment since then.

Då blir barna fulla med sommar, och bena blir
fulla med spring.

Ms. Gustavsen has tears in her eyes when we're finally done.

"Your singing has really improved," she says, her voice cracking a bit. "And that makes me so happy. It truly warms the cockles of my heart!"

Olivia and Emma laugh and squirm. Marcus smiles at them and rolls his eyes. They roll theirs back and giggle even more. Then Ms. Gustavsen shouts that there are only ten minutes left of sixth grade and that we need to line up so she can say goodbye before we all leave.

I manage to get a place right behind Marcus. I have to push Joanna a little to make it happen. Once again

I can see his back and his head and his shiny hair. His red T-shirt and tan arms. He has his own smell. I lean forward and take a breath. It smells like boy and laundry detergent, maybe some sunscreen.

Ms. Gustavsen starts a kind of ceremony where she gives everyone a hug, a handshake, a look right in the eye, and a "have a nice summer." It takes a while. Luckily. I'm perfectly positioned a bit too close to Marcus. I make sure my arm brushes against his arm, that my cheek grazes his back. These are the last seconds before I won't get to see him for millions of seconds. After all, he'll barely be home, so I probably won't run into him. He lives far away anyway. I've walked past his house loads of times, though. His room is on the second floor, with Chelsea curtains in the window.

Ms. Gustavsen gives Marcus a hug. His tan arms wrap around her neck. Imagine if it were *me* he was hugging. Imagine if *I* were Ms. Gustavsen right now.

"And you have a great summer, Nora."

Suddenly Ms. Gustavsen is right next to my face.

"I hope you have a great vacation," she says, hugging me hard.

She looks at me for a long time, staring at me properly, like there's something she wants to say to me that she can't get out.

"You, too," I say. "I'm sure it'll be nice out in the woods."

Ms. Gustavsen winks at me. Then she continues. And that's when I notice Wilmer. He's standing right behind me and says he's excited to start in this class. It seems like there are some really nice people here, I can hear him saying to Ms. Gustavsen. This seems so weird that I have to turn to look at him. Either he's an idiot, or just a little too optimistic.

"Maybe I'll see you around," he says to me suddenly.

And now I decide. That crooked front tooth *is* ugly. There isn't anything charming about those kinds of crooked teeth. He just looks lame. Why would he see me around? I turn and look at Marcus again. I can't be bothered to be nice to Wilmer just because he's new and is going to be at home all summer.

The whole class is standing in a row as we chatter and laugh and mess around and wait. Wait for the signal that now, *now* Ms. Gustavsen is done with her hugging, *now* it's summer vacation—fifty-four days off. What we've been waiting for the whole school year.

And then it happens.

"Have a great summer, 6A!" Ms. Gustavsen shouts as loud as she can, throwing her arms in the air like a circus ringmaster.

And the classroom erupts. Twenty-six sixth graders shoot like red-hot lava out into summer vacation. We run out the door, down the hall, down the stairs, through the doors, and out into the sunny schoolyard. Shouting and shrieking and cheering. It's summer. It's vacation. All there is to do is get going with your plans. If you have any.

A group of kids is gathered by the school gate. People who were running out to vacation only two minutes before are now sweating and out of breath, blocking the exit so it's impossible to start summer before you've pushed past. Olivia's blonde head sticks up in the middle. Her voice is loud and shrill, as though she's were giving the last vital instructions to a troop of soldiers going to war. Marcus is standing next to her, listening attentively.

"It starts at six o'clock," Olivia commands. "And *everyone* has to come!"

I hesitate for a moment. I look around, but there's no choice but to gather here with the rest. Otherwise, I'd have to jump over the fence, and that would attract even more attention than if I just melt in silently at the very back.

Then I remember the invitation and the pictures of Olivia on the card—in a bathing suit and sunglasses, on a boat and at the beach, an ice cream in her hand. She's smiling happily in every single one. The invitation is still in my bag. I didn't even check what day it would be. I usually don't go to birthday parties, since Mom gets so stressed out about gifts. I hadn't planned on going to this one, either. *Especially* not this one.

The group disperses, and people start spreading out onto the street.

"You're coming too, right?"

Olivia is suddenly standing right in front of me. Emma is next to her.

I hesitate. A thousand excuses race through my head.

"I'm leaving pretty early tomorrow morning," I can hear myself answering.

Marcus comes over. He smiles. That red T-shirt and those tan arms. The smell of sunscreen and fabric softener. He's standing so close it makes me nervous. I've only spoken to him a few times, and one of those times was when we had a group project about vitamin D, so that doesn't even count. Now I hurry to put my hands in the pockets of my shorts, just to be sure of where they are and to be certain that they behave. He's smiling. Oh my God, he's smiling. And I smile back. At least I *think* I do. My lips are pressing against each other, and my face muscles are sore after about two seconds.

"When does your flight leave?" he asks.

He's talking to me! He's wondering about something in my life!

"Five thirty," I answer quickly, and an intense heat spreads across my cheeks. "And there's a lot to pack since we're going to be gone for so long."

If I look up, I could look in his eyes properly, but I don't dare. Last night, right before I was going to bed, I thought that the worst part of the fifty-four days of summer break was the fact that I wouldn't see Marcus that whole time. There's a lot of other things that suck, too, but not seeing Marcus is probably the worst. I look down at the ground and feel my hands sweating in my pockets, and I'm positive I'm just as red as the T-shirt in front of me.

"But I'm guessing you don't go to bed at six?"

Olivia and Emma giggle. He smiles at the two girls, then at me. Marcus is going to the party—of course he is. *Everyone* is going to the party. *Everyone* wants to go to the party.

"So you're coming, then," Olivia says firmly.

"Yeah," I reply, and look down, waiting for Marcus to say that it's great that I'm coming. As if he would ever think such a thing *and* say it in front of both Olivia and Emma.

"What's up?" says a voice from behind us.

It's him again. Wilmer with the front tooth. Where did he even come from, actually?

Wilmer smiles at the two girls, then at me. He raises

his eyebrows to emphasize that he's just asked us something. I look at Marcus. At his lovely face. And then I roll my eyes. Because Wilmer just seems *way* too curious.

"I'm having a birthday party tonight," Olivia says. "For the whole class."

"That's so cool," Wilmer says enthusiastically.

It seems like he's just assuming he's invited. Even though we just met him today and he made a pretty bad first impression with his ugly clothes and no plans for vacation.

"Maybe we can go together?" he asks, looking at me like it's a normal thing to suggest. "Since you know where people in our class live," he adds.

Olivia and Emma look at each other. Marcus looks at me. It looks like all three of them might start laughing at any second. For a tiny moment, it seemed like this was going to go well . . . until Wilmer came along and got all mixed up in it. I roll my eyes again, just to emphasize that Wilmer is being pushy, that he absolutely *isn't* friend material. Now we're suddenly the two weirdos who live in Craplin and belong together. And if there's something I'm not on board with, it's exactly that.

"See you at six," Olivia says, swallowing an outburst of laughter.

The three of them walk off in the same direction, to the right toward Solvang Heights, where they all live.

I can tell that Wilmer's looking at me, but I just start walking. As fast as I can. To the left, toward Chaplin Court. Without responding to him. Wilmer is sticking to me like glue.

I will absolutely *not* walk together with you, I think as I stomp home.

t's quiet and hot back at the apartment. Stuffy. The windows are all shut, and the sun is blazing into the living room. A couple of brown plants on the windowsill look thirsty. Some withered daisies are drooping in a vase. A pillar of dust swirls in the sunlight. The door to Mom's room is ajar, the duvet is crumpled up, and it takes a couple of seconds before I realize she isn't lying there. She's usually home when I come back from school—and usually asleep. I can't remember her saying she'd be doing anything today.

Mom's been tired for a while. Maybe since November. Since before last Christmas, at least, but I haven't counted the exact number of days. "It'll pass soon," she says about every other day, smiling optimistically with her sleepy brown eyes. "Things work out for smart girls, Nora."

I open the window in my room and lie down on the bed. Some kids are playing out in the backyard, laughing and shrieking like a couple of seagulls competing for who can scream the loudest.

Olivia's birthday party. She handed out the invitations weeks ago and told everyone they *had* to keep the date free.

Should I go? I hadn't been planning on it. You have to bring a present to birthday parties, and those obviously cost money, which is hard to get without asking Mom. And Mom always gets so stressed when I ask questions about money. So I normally say I'm sick or I'm doing something else or I'm gone that day. Thanks for the invitation, but unfortunately, I can't come.

Marcus is going. My upper lip is sweaty. Partly because of the stuffy air but mostly because of Marcus. If I go to Olivia's party, I'll get two more hours with Marcus before the fifty-four days begin.

I call Mom, but it goes straight to voicemail and her tired voice. "You've reached Anja. Leave a message after the beep." I hang up and go into the kitchen, open the fridge, and look at the shelves. A jar of strawberry jam, half a pizza, ketchup, and some mayo. Maybe Mom's at the store.

I eat the cold pizza and look out the window at the backyard. I think about the tropics. About Marcus. About the birthday party. And I decide to go.

I Google "birthday + twelve years old + girl + gift + price." I change my mind and eat some jam on toast as I text Mom in caps: *WHERE ARE YOU?*

Sometimes there's money in a box in the kitchen cupboard. A dollar or five, or maybe even a twenty. I look in the cupboard. Mom might not even notice if some is missing.

The box is annoyingly light. It makes a feeble clinking noise when I shake it. You can't go to a birthday party without a present. I toss the box back in the cupboard.

Then I see it. A note on the kitchen table, a bit under the tablecloth. It's weird I didn't notice it before, that I sat there and ate half a pizza without even seeing the piece of paper with Mom's handwriting. It says she's at class and that she'll be home around six. We can eat tacos for dinner tonight. And she drew a heart. It's crooked and looks weird. Inside the heart it says "Nora."

I think for twenty seconds and then I text her again. I write that she doesn't need to buy stuff for tacos because I'm going to a birthday party. Then I delete that and change it to "class party" before I press send. Class parties are good. Class parties are free.

I wait a bit for her to answer, but nothing happens. I almost change my mind again, but then I close my eyes and imagine Marcus in his red T-shirt. When I open my eyes again, I've decided. For real. I have a plan.

livia lives in a white house with a garden and shrubs and big windows and a mom who's welcoming everyone in. Her mom is wearing tight white pants and has red nails, big teeth, and blonde hair in a ponytail. Sunglasses on top of her head. Gold earrings. She doesn't seem tired at all. She actually seems happy.

"It's so nice to see you, Nora," she says, giving me a hug.

She smells like perfume. Sweet and feminine and not as strong as Ms. Gustavsen's. It's amazing that she knows the name of everyone in Olivia's class. She knows my name is Nora, even though I've only been in the class for a year and even though Olivia and I aren't exactly *friends*. She's the kind of person who keeps up with things. Who reads mail. Who goes to parent-teacher conferences. Who memorizes names and is completely tuned in.

"Hi . . . there," I say as she's hugging me, feeling a bit weird that this woman I don't even know seems to know my name.

A lot of people have already arrived. Some are out on the terrace, some are inside. I look for Marcus—isn't he here yet? Olivia comes out in a light-purple dress. Her hair is hanging down over her shoulders in big waves. She probably spent about four hours with a curling iron. At least.

I can hear Wilmer introducing himself to Olivia's mom behind me. He's new to the class, he says, but he hopes it's okay that he came to the party anyway.

Wilmer was standing in the backyard when I left for the party, but I acted like I didn't see him. He was ten feet behind me all the way here.

I walk toward the terrace, practicing my plan. I keep looking for Marcus but he's nowhere to be seen. He *has* to be here. It's all a waste of time if he doesn't come. If he only knew what I was risking for his sake.

"Hiiiii," says Olivia.

She hugs me tightly like we're best friends and like she wouldn't have survived this party if I hadn't shown up. Then she looks at me. Waiting.

And it's then that I put the plan into motion.

"Oh my God!" I shout so loudly that it catches most people's attention. "The present! I forgot your present! Is that even possible? Oh my God, I'm such an idiot!"

Olivia looks at me.

"You forgot my present?" she asks, disappointed.

I nod and look as sad as I possibly can. I can almost feel the tears coming out.

"I spent *so* much time finding exactly the right gift," I say.

"Nora forgot my present," Olivia says dejectedly to Emma, who's suddenly shown up.

Emma looks at me like I'm a virus that's planning on infecting everyone at the party.

"Should I go home and get it, or . . . ?" I ask meekly.

I don't know why I suggested that. If she says yes, then I have a big problem. What is it that I'm supposed to have spent so much time buying for Olivia? I can feel my fingers automatically crossing as a kind of last cry for help. *Please*, don't make me have to go home to get something that doesn't exist. *Please*, just let me be at a party with Marcus.

Olivia and Emma look at each other. There's a pile of presents on a table right inside the terrace door. She can't possibly need one more.

"Everyone can forget things."

It's Olivia's mom, smiling at me kindly.

"Olivia can come and pick up the present from you another day. Don't worry about it, Nora."

She pats me lightly on the back and shouts that everyone has to come into the living room. It's time to open presents.

Olivia's living room is bigger than my whole apartment. A huge table is covered with a tablecloth and place cards and flower arrangements. There are silver balloons in the window that spell out OLIVIA 12 YEARS OLD, one balloon for every letter and number. There's an enormous cake in the middle of the table.

Olivia tells us to make a circle. She sits down in the middle and then picks up each package one by one, reading aloud from the cards before opening the gifts. More and more and more. There are purses and makeup. Envelopes with cash. A twenty or a fifty. Olivia shows how much she's gotten and shouts out a thank you to everyone. Her dad gathers the bills so they won't get lost in the pile of wrapping paper.

Olivia's mom claps her hands and says we should take our seats.

"Who wants pizza?" she sings.

And then all of a sudden, while everyone is buzzing around and reading the place cards to find out where they're sitting, he's standing there. In blue shorts and a white T-shirt. His dreamy brown eyes are smiling. My stomach starts pounding, or maybe it's my heart. Because he's *here*. He doesn't see me, but he's here, in the same room. Marcus gives Olivia a hug. He's sitting next to her at the head of the table, far away from me. I have a place at the very end, next to Joanna, but at least I have a place. Wilmer just stands next to the table looking stupid. No one thought about making a place card for the new boy. Olivia's mom scurries over with a glass and plate and apologizes at least four times.

It's hard to eat pizza, talk to Joanna, and look at Marcus at the same time. Luckily, Joanna talks a *lot*. If I concentrate on saying yes and no and ooh and huh while she's talking, a lot of the work is already done. Marcus folds his pizza slices and chews vigorously. He dabs his mouth with his napkin, chats, and laughs. It's impossible to hear what they're talking about over there, but Olivia is clearly being funny. It seems like he thinks she looks pretty, too, with her curls and purple dress. He leans toward her more than once. Joanna tells me about a boathouse in northern Norway and how she's going to go canoeing for the first time. It's insanely boring, but I smile anyway, just in case Marcus suddenly looks over. Something he'll *never* do. Wilmer is now sitting right across from me. He's smiling and it seems like he's having fun. He tells us about a time he and his dad went on a fishing trip like it worked well with Joanna's stories about canoeing.

"Fourteen flounders," he says proudly, and tells us that his dad lost the bet and had to go swimming with all his clothes on.

They're having tons of fun at the head of the table. I would've done anything to be sitting there, but I'm stuck here. Far away from everything. I need friends who lift me up, not people who want to talk about flounders and canoeing. I look over at the other end of the table and think that something really *has* to change. Olivia is taking a selfie with Marcus. I simply can't eat any more pizza. It's quiet down at our end of the table, apart from Wilmer, who's still laughing at his own fishing story and shoveling in yet another slice of pizza.

I've been here for an hour and forty minutes without talking to Marcus. I've lied about a gift and tried to act interested in canoeing and flounders, but he hasn't even noticed I'm here.

I look at the clock. Even though summer vacation has way too many hours and minutes without Marcus, I'm actually pretty happy to see that there are only twenty minutes left of this party.

"Did you figure out which country you're going to, then?" Emma asks while we're sitting on a gigantic couch during the last few minutes of the party. "Or are you still going to *the tropics*?"

She says "the tropics" in an exaggerated and sarcastic way, giggling and looking at Olivia. There are a few people listening, but then again there are *always* people listening when Emma and Olivia are talking.

"My mom was at class," I say. "So I couldn't ask."

Olivia and Emma laugh again. Quietly and irritatingly.

I haven't said much during this party, but now it happens all at once. I start babbling. About the pools, about the apartment we're staying in. Or the *bungalow*, as it's called. It's right on the beach, which is long and white and full of palm trees.

"There are waterslides, too," I say. "Which look *super* cool. And there's a spa area and tons of shops nearby, so we'll probably do a lot of shopping as well."

There are more people looking at me now. Marcus, too.

"And luckily it's all-inclusive," I continue. "So you can eat as much as you want all day. But we'll go to restaurants sometimes, too, when we get sick of eating at the hotel."

I smile.

"I'm going to get super tan," I brag. "We're going to be there for weeks. Five or six, I think. And we're just going to relax."

I suddenly see Olivia whispering something to Emma. Emma smiles.

"You have to remember to send pictures, then," she says.

I swallow and nod.

"We're excited to see them," says Olivia.

I nod again and look down at the floor. I can hear Olivia telling everyone to post lots of pictures from their vacations on Instagram, so everyone can see them. My pulse beats in my temples. Now I have a new problem. Can I forget my phone? While I'm on vacation for weeks?

Luckily, Olivia's mom interrupts.

"Now the party has unfortunately come to an end," she says. "Thank you to everyone for coming and have a wonderful summer!"

Olivia stands in the doorway to hug everyone before we leave. She says thank you for all the nice presents. Her mom and dad are standing behind her, smiling. I give her a quick hug and don't say a word about the present I unfortunately forgot. Marcus is at the very back of the line. I walk as slowly as I can, turning around about every third step to see if he isn't coming soon. And when I'm all the way by the gate, I see it: Olivia kissing Marcus on the cheek. I'm 98 percent sure that it was a kiss.

Summer vacation *definitely* could've started better. For example, it could have been *me* kissing Marcus on the cheek. He could have even walked me home after the party. Maybe not all the way to my neighborhood and apartment, but at least to the traffic light by the store, then I could walk the rest of the way by myself. Across the street, through the gate, into the backyard, and over to Building A. And then before I went up to the third floor, I could take out my phone and send him a text, or just an emoji heart, or something like that. Maybe Marcus would have time to see me once during the seventy-seven thousand hours that are summer vacation. Or we could go to the beach. Or go on a bike ride. Even though he's going to the south of France and Spain and London.

Mom is sitting in the living room when I go in. She gets up, turns off the TV, and comes over to me in the hallway. She pushes her hair back and tries to hide a yawn. Her sweatpants are stained and she's wearing a pair of blue slippers.

"Did you have fun?" she asks in a quiet, tired voice.

"Yeah," I lie, letting her give me a hug.

"I guess you ate there?" Mom asks.

I nod. Even though I'm a little hungry, food doesn't exactly seem tempting after what I've just gone through.

"I'm going to bed a little early tonight," Mom says.

As if this is big news. Why does she feel like she has to inform me about this every single night? That she's going to bed early?

"It's Friday," I reply.

Mom nods, leaning against the doorframe.

"But I've been at class," she says, "and it really wore me out."

I want to tell her that it's normal to have a job when you're grown up, that other grown-ups get up early and go to work, that they make dinner and watch the news. That they wear white pants and have ponytails and know what their kids' friends' names are. That they plan birthday parties for the whole class. But I don't have the energy. Not now.

"Do we have any candy?" I ask, even though I've been eating cake and candy all night.

"No," she replies. "I haven't had the chance to go to the store yet. I was at class."

I roll my eyes. I know it will upset her, but at this point that *class* is really starting to bug me.

"We can do something fun tomorrow," Mom says. "I don't have my class then."

Is this really happening? I've had enough of this stupid class! What does she even go to a class to learn? Italian? Knitting? The tango? I can't imagine a single class that would suit Mom, except for a class about being a better mom.

"What's this class even about?" I ask.

"Ah, well," Mom answers. "Sit down for a sec, Nora."

She shuffles over to the couch. I sit down next to her and look at the sharp lines in her face, her colorless lips, her dry hair. What's going on? Mom looks serious. Like "we need to have a talk" serious. She takes a breath and lets it all out with a kind of whistle before she starts to talk.

"It's a class I . . . have to take. To try to get a job. But I'm really not in a good place right now. I can already tell that it's going to be really hard."

I think about regular grown-ups again. Grown-ups who both work *and* go take classes.

"And I learned something today that's a bit of a bummer," Mom continues. "The class is actually six weeks long."

"Six weeks?!" I shout.

Mom nods dejectedly.

"And you think that's a *bit* of a bummer?"

"I told them I have a kid and that it's the start of summer break, but I've been putting it off for so long that now I just have to go, or else we won't get any unemployment money."

Mom looks down and blinks uncontrollably. What does she mean? *Or else* we won't get any money.

"I guess it'll be a little bit boring for you . . ." she says, looking up at me uncertainly.

Half an hour ago, I didn't think summer break could get any worse, but I was wrong. Summer break can *clearly* get worse.

"But I talked to Grandma, and she said you can go to her place sometimes, or at least call her so you feel like you have a grown-up nearby."

Nearby? It takes over twenty minutes to bike to Grandma's, and that's if you bike fast. And then what am I supposed to even do at Grandma's? Read magazines and watch TV and knit?

I don't say anything.

"There must be a lot of others who'll be at home, too."

Mom really has no clue. If only she knew what the people in my class were doing on their summer breaks.

"Maria, for example. You can hang out with her?"

I look down.

"And there are so many places close by you can bike to, like the beach."

She groans wearily.

"We just have to make the best of it," Mom says meekly. "And we can do things together in the afternoons when I'm done with my class."

I don't want to answer. I know she's lying. When she's done with her class, she's going to come straight home and go to sleep. She isn't going to have the energy to do anything at all.

"I'm doing the best that I can," she says softly, almost so I can't even hear her.

She always says that, maybe to comfort herself. As if being a mom is so insanely difficult that hardly anyone manages to do it properly.

Now I look at her and get up from the couch. I *hate* this class. I *hate* this summer break. I *hate* Marcus. And Olivia. And vacation plans.

"What are you doing?" Mom asks uneasily.

My stomach and head are pounding and burning. I want to open the window and throw everything out, hurl it all into the backyard. The couch, the curtains, the dry plants on the windowsill, the picture of me and Mom on the wall, the box in the kitchen cabinet with nothing more than a couple of dimes, the chairs, the tablecloth, Mom. Everything.

"*I'M GOING TO THE TROPICS!*" I shout and run out of the living room and into the hallway. I yank open the door to my room and slam it so hard the wall shakes. I throw myself onto my bed and bite down on the duvet.

"To the tropics," I sob into the duvet cover, and my heart feels like it's breaking.

The beach is long and white, the ocean blue, almost turquoise. A light breeze makes lying on the beach chair bearable. It gently caresses my warm, tan skin. The sound of birds chirping and children playing. Waves lapping. Summery music from the beach bar. I'll go for a swim before lunch, I think. Maybe I'll have an ice cream, too. I can pretty much do whatever I want—that's what's so nice. I don't have to worry about anything, I only have absolutely everything to look forward to. I have a sweet, pink drink on the ground, with a straw so long I don't even have to lean over. A yellow umbrella adorns the top of the glass. There are seven pools and several waterslides. A pool with pirate ships is a big hit with the little kids. In the "relax" pool, the pace is slower, and the atmosphere is more relaxed. The bungalows are tastefully decorated and have a view of the ocean. There's pretty much everything you could ever ask for on a dream vacation here.

That's what it says. The pictures are beautiful. Bright

and summery, so you can almost feel the sun and the ocean and the sand just by looking at them. At least if you look long enough. Just like I am.

There's a heat wave during the first days of summer break—it's probably about a hundred and fifty degrees in the apartment. I don't dare open the windows facing the street in case someone from my class walks past and wonders why we're airing out the apartment while we're in the tropics. I'm not as concerned with the windows to the backyard. I open them as wide as possible every single day after Mom leaves for her class, but the air is still stifling inside the apartment. I sit there sweating like any other tropical tourist.

I call Grandma every day after Mom has left. I tell her it's so hot there's only one thing to do: go to the beach and hang out there until Mom comes home again. Maybe I can come visit her on a day it's a little cooler, I say, trying to sound happy.

"Of course you want to be with your friends," Grandma says. "I was out in the country all summer when I was younger and we were out and about all day. There weren't any adults who had time to watch us."

Grandma laughs into the phone.

"Have fun, sweetie," she says.

And then we hang up.

I spend a lot of time in the tropics. I look and look for the perfect place for me and Mom. I put in the criteria: pool, balcony, ocean views, all-inclusive, waterslides. I sort by price and choose the most expensive, the one with the most stars: *Blue Lagoon Deluxe*. We'll stay in the suite right on the beach, the one with its own pool on the terrace, just in case we get tired of swimming with everyone else. The man at reception looks nice. The woman at the beach bar smiles in a pink T-shirt, holding up a glass crammed with umbrellas and straws. Two women with long brown hair and a lot of makeup work in the spa section. They're smiling, too. Everyone smiles in the tropics.

Mom changes into sweats as soon as she comes home in the afternoon. She says the class is incredibly tiring and that she doesn't have the energy to do anything. She asks the same questions every single day before she has to go lie down to rest:

"Have you had a nice day? Have you been out?"

I say yes, even though it's a lie. Mom is so happy when she hears I've been out. That's what you're *supposed* to do when it's summer break. Then I ask two questions back:

"Did you have a good time at your class? Did you learn anything?"

Mom answers no to both, and then the conversation is over.

In the evening, we make frozen pizza for dinner, and Mom often talks about shrimp. She *really* wants shrimp. She *dreams* about shrimp, has plans for shrimp—as soon as she has a little extra money. After all, that's what you eat in the summer: shrimp. And you drink white wine. On the beach or on a veranda or on a boat.

"You're not supposed to sit inside and eat frozen pizza," Mom says dejectedly in her sweatpants.

I say that pizza's fine. We don't need shrimp.

"Oh, honey," Mom says, her mouth full of pizza. "This isn't exactly a dream summer, I guess."

She looks out the window at the gray backyard of our apartment complex.

"I guess shrimp won't really help much, anyway," she mumbles.

Chaplin is an ugly apartment complex. There's a narrow strip of grass at one end of the backyard, but otherwise, it's just asphalt. There's an area in the middle of the backyard with some clotheslines that no one uses to dry their clothes. The lines just drape there loosely. Right next to that are the garbage cans—green plastic boxes that are often overflowing with bags, so the lids are always propped open. In the mornings there's always a mess of leftover food and paper and plastic bags that have been pecked open by birds. Next to the clotheslines there's a sandbox full of leaves that always smells like cat pee. Spread across the rest of the backyard is a playset, with swings and a seesaw that's rusty and creaks whenever someone uses it, which fortunately isn't very often, even though there are tons of kids who live here.

The brick buildings are painted yellow, and there are patches where the paint is peeling off and you can see gray cement underneath. There are four stories, and doors to the different stairwells around the whole backyard. At the top is *A*, where we live, and then it goes down in alphabetical order, all the way to *J*. There are a lot of doors. Ten, to be precise.

Our stairwell is green, which means that it's always dark in there. And there must be something wrong with the ceiling lamp since it's always flickering. Dark, light, dark, light.

"How long are we going to live here?" I asked Mom when we first moved in.

I liked where we lived before much better. We had a balcony and a view of a park. Now we have a view of the backyard from the kitchen and my room. From the living room, we look out onto the street and right down to a gas station that's always open. And *very* frequently used.

"I don't really know," Mom said. "But probably a while."

On the very first day of my new class, I did something stupid. I was asked to say my name, where I live, and what I like to do in my free time. So I said my name was Nora and skipped over the thing about my free time since I didn't really know what I should say about that. Then I said that I'd moved into 30 Miller Avenue, and someone in the class, I think it was Emma, asked if that was Chaplin, and I said yes. Because I didn't know any better. That was before I realized that I should *never* say

I live in Chaplin if anyone asks. A few people snickered, and then I heard it for the very first time. My new home's nickname. *Craplin* Court.

Now I say that I live in Solvang Heights, an area just past Chaplin, so it's almost not lying. Solvang Heights has nice houses with gravel and gardens and garages. Playgrounds with new playsets and seesaws that don't creak.

The name Craplin suits Chaplin. Now I've been living here one fall and one winter and one spring and soon one summer, and it's just as ugly here no matter what season it is. There's a sign that says WELCOME TO CHAPLIN COURT, but someone scratched off the *CH* and wrote *CR* in big black letters. No one has bothered to wash it off.

It sucks to be on vacation in Craplin Court. Because that is basically what I'm doing. I can't go out, in case I see someone. So I have to sit inside. Like a prisoner.

here are four million six hundred and sixty-five thousand six hundred seconds in summer break. I've spent twenty-five of them calculating this number. I don't know how many seconds I've spent on YouTube, but I've probably watched about two hundred and eighty-five videos of people making slime. It's a shame I'm in the tropics and can't go out to buy contact lens solution and shaving cream to make my own.

I Google "prisoner + own home" and read stories about other people in the same boat as me. Prisoners serving time at home with ankle monitors. A depressed mother with a baby who feels trapped at home and doesn't have the energy to take the baby out. A poet who hasn't left his apartment for thirty years. There are a lot of us who are trapped in our own homes in different ways. I make up stories about why I'm a prisoner. It feels good to lie a little when the truth is as embarrassing as it is.

In addition to becoming a slime expert, I've spent a

lot of time visiting Blue Lagoon Deluxe. I've given every-one in the pictures names so it's almost like I know them. Monica and Eliza in the spa. Dori with the tall chef's hat. Jonathan and Alexandra at the front desk. Leandra in the kids' club and Margarita with the umbrella drinks. This has used up a few thousand seconds. It takes time to make up good names.

I spend a lot of time counting. It's pointless knowing how many forks are in the drawer. How many pairs of underwear I have, or how many cars fill up at the gas station over the course of one morning. How many pic-tures have been posted on our class group.

Olivia posts photos from the resort in Portugal. She's already gotten super tan and is smiling at the camera, her hair blowing to one side. Emma shares pictures from Paris, standing in front of the Eiffel Tower, eating ice cream, with enormous shopping bags in her hands. *Have fun*, Olivia writes. Julie posts pictures from Cyprus. The beach is white and the ocean is turquoise and she's wear-ing a bikini and sunglasses. She writes that she's having a great time. Marcus is sitting in a big boat. He's probably the only person in the whole world who looks good in a life jacket. His eyes are closed, and the sun is shining on his face, and he's even tanner than he was on the last day of school. Joanna shares pictures from the boathouse in northern Norway. She hasn't gotten as many likes as the others, and no one has commented on what she posted.

I can't stop looking at the pictures. There are new ones every day, several times a day. There's always sun. They're *always* having fun. No one is bored, no one is arguing, and no one is angry. There isn't a cloud in the sky. And luckily, no one has asked for pictures from my trip to the tropics.

I'm already dreading school starting again because we'll have to talk about our vacation. Everyone *has* to talk about what a nice a time they had. Everyone *has* to have had a nice time.

Something *has* to happen, I think. Because this is the *worst* tropical vacation I've ever been on. And I've never even been to the tropics.

Then something happens.

I'm eating dinner with Mom in the kitchen. She's sitting with her feet curled up under her on the kitchen chair and slurping from a cup of tea. Her sweatpants are more stained than ever and she smiles weakly.

"I spoke with Grandma earlier. She said you're so busy you haven't had time to visit her."

"Yeah," I lie.

I've watched twenty-three videos about slime today, but I tell her I was at the beach.

"How was the water?" she asks.

"Cold," I answer quickly.

I don't *have* to go into detail.

"Were you by yourself?"

"No," I lie again. "I went with Maria."

Mom smiles at me. I make it sound nice. Who *wouldn't* want to go to the beach with Maria, you know? Best friends on the beach all day.

"You should invite her here someday," Mom says. "I'd love to meet her."

I look at Mom and nod. My chest is pounding, right under my heart. It tingles.

"Maybe she likes shrimp," Mom says, and I nod again.

"I can ask," I say, putting my hand on the leg that's started shaking.

"That would be nice," Mom says dreamily. "A proper shrimp dinner. You and me and Maria."

I nod for the third time. We have to talk about something else. I can't tell her about Maria, not now. I look at Mom.

"If you could travel anywhere in the world on vacation with me, where would you want to go?"

Mom smiles. She likes this kind of question. She wrinkles her forehead and it looks like she's thinking hard, deliberating.

"The tropics," she says firmly.

"The tropics?"

"Yes. Somewhere where there's sun and sand and it's warm and we don't have to think about anything at all, just have fun."

Blue Lagoon Deluxe. Me and Mom in the big suite.

"You know the tropics aren't a country," I say teasingly.

She laughs.

"But you know what I mean, Nora. I'm talking about

the Caribbean, Brazil . . . It's all the same to me, as long as it's the tropics."

I know what she means. No one knows better than me.

I feel happy when I go to bed, the taste of toothpaste in my mouth and wearing a clean nightgown. Mom is watching TV in the living room. We ate potato chips and drank soda, even though it's a weekday. Mom probably talked for twenty minutes about what she'd do if she won a million dollars in the lottery.

It's still light out and a reddish-pink sun is just setting over Building F. I stand by the window and look out into the backyard. My window is open a crack and the warm evening air seeps into my room.

And that's when it happens. Right as the sun disappears behind the roof.

"Nora?"

The voice is coming from the backyard. I freeze. I can't breathe.

"Nora?"

There's something familiar about the voice, but I can't manage to place it. It sounds like a boy.

"Hello?"

I back up into my room and crouch down. I crawl toward my bed so the person who's clearly seen me in the window won't see me again.

"Nora?"

My stomach pounds. My chest prickles. I turn off the light over my bed, the only light that's in my room. But it doesn't get dark. It's the lightest month of the year. You can still see *everything*. I peek out the window.

And then I see it—who's shouting. He's standing down in the backyard and peering up at my window: a boy in a blue T-shirt with curly hair.

He's seen me! I've been exposed. I should've kept this window closed, too. I'd forgotten he lived right across from me.

Wilmer. The most annoying neighbor in the world. Now he knows I'm not in the tropics.

I wake up the next day drenched in sweat. I slept with my window closed, and it must be about two hundred degrees in my room. I drew the curtains, too. I'm trying to make it look like it's empty here, even though Wilmer's already seen me.

I'd been thinking of venturing out and biking to Grandma's today. Yesterday I found an enormous straw hat in Mom's closet and stood in front of the mirror for a long time. I tried to decide if it was enough to disguise me if I pulled the hat all the way down my forehead. But after the thing with Wilmer, I'm not taking any chances. I call Grandma and tell her I'm going to Maria's.

"Of course, my dear," Grandma says, and she sounds happy.

She completely understands that I want to spend time with Maria instead of her.

"This isn't exactly a dream summer for you, is it?" she says, and she sounds just like Mom. Have they been practicing this line together?

"But I think it's great that you're out and about so much. You're making the best out of the situation, and that's a great quality, sweetie."

It's weird how everyone thinks I'm doing so great. I must be doing a really good job of lying, I guess. What would Grandma say if I told her everything? That I'm just making up my life. Grandma loves that I have so many friends, that I'm always busy, just like she was when she was a kid. Grandma likes *normal* things. She doesn't like talking about anything sad. When Mom got tired and lost her job and we had to move to Chaplin, Grandma was so angry because we lived even further away than before. She rarely comes to visit, and if she does come, it always ends with Mom crying when she leaves. Grandma likes when things are good.

"Have fun," she says, and hangs up.

Wilmer is standing out in the backyard again that night. I can hear him shouting my name at my window, which is closed, of course. I sit in the dark in my room, completely still on my bed. I don't dare move in case Wilmer has X-ray vision and can see through the wall. My hairline is dripping with sweat, and my top is plastered to my back. He shouts my name four times. Then it's quiet. I've just gotten up from my bed when I hear a new sound. There's a tapping noise against my window. Several times. I don't manage to count how many. I lean toward the window and carefully push the curtain to one side so I can look out with one eye. He's throwing with all his might so the tiny pebbles will make it all the way up to the third floor. It looks almost comical.

After a while, he gives up and goes back toward Building F. A few minutes later, a light comes on in a window on the third floor, straight across from me. I sit in the dark and look at him through a crack in the curtains. He's sitting there, staring at his computer. Quiet and alone. Like me.

keep the window closed and the curtains drawn over the next few days, just to be on the safe side. If vacation sucked before, it's gotten even worse now. I sit in my boiling-hot apartment and hate the tropics. I hate myself for lying. Why couldn't I just have done the same as Wilmer? I didn't *have* to say that Mom is broke. I could've just said we were going to hang out at home. Maybe I could've even pretended that was at the top of our wish list for the summer.

Emma is in the Canary Islands now. Almost everyone in our class likes the pictures she posted of herself in front of the big pool. Julie is holding a French flag and is leaning against a wall full of purple flowers. Everyone in our class likes her picture, too. Marcus is swimming with his brothers on a sandy beach in Spain. Olivia commented with a heart. Maybe it's the heat, the stuffy air, the bone-dry plants, and the sight of all the pictures that make me go crazy, but suddenly something happens that I don't have any control over. I copy the pictures from

Blue Lagoon Deluxe, choose one of the pool under a sparkling sun, and open up Instagram. *Having fun*, I write. And post. Before I can even think twice.

Nothing happens for a few minutes. I sit there with my phone in my hand, clutching it, staring at no likes and no comments. I regret having posted anything at all. But then it happens. *Looks so nice*, Joanna writes. *Have fun*, writes Alexandra. Theo sends a sun. Several people like the picture. But not Olivia. Not Emma. And not Marcus.

Wilmer throws more pebbles at my window. Every single night. I lie there in bed and count the number of taps against my window. One night it's eight. Another seventeen. I wonder what he's thinking, why he's still doing this. I realized a while ago that Wilmer is lacking normal social skills, but this confirms it even more. When he finally gives up, I watch him through the crack in the curtains. The light in his apartment turns on and I can see his head in the window, his curls. I like looking at him over there. I don't really know why. He sits in an office chair in what must be his room. The walls are light blue, and nothing is hanging on them. It looks like he's playing on his computer.

Tonight, I count nine taps. Then it's quiet. I look out of the crack in the curtains. He turns on the light in his room, stands in the window, and looks straight at me. It's after eleven. Mom is using her electric toothbrush in the bathroom. And then I hear it. A weak sound from my phone. The message is from an unknown number. Five words and a question mark. *What happened to the tropics?*

I wake up early the next day. I can hear Mom putting on the kettle and rattling the cups while the radio plays opera. I check my phone to be sure that I didn't just dream it, but the message is still there.

Mom is sitting by the kitchen table, slurping tea and chewing on a piece of toast with strawberry jam.

"So, did he call you yesterday?" she asks as I come into the kitchen. "What was his name again?"

I gape at her. I probably look like an alien who landed on earth five minutes ago and doesn't understand a single thing that's happening.

"A boy called me yesterday and asked for your number," Mom says, smiling with jam on her teeth. "He's starting in your class in the fall and wanted to get to know you a bit before school starts."

Wilmer. I knew it was him as soon as I saw the message yesterday.

"He seemed really nice," Mom continues. "A perky kid. Polite."

She takes a big bite and keeps talking with food in her mouth.

"I can't remember his name. It was something kind of unusual."

I don't say the name. I just say that no one called. I quickly try to change the subject and talk about my plans for the day instead. Maria and I are going on a bike ride. Mom smiles even more. The perfect daughter, who knows how to make the most of what wasn't exactly a dream summer.

"And I have to get off to my class," she says, and for the first time, she sounds cheerful when she says the word *class*.

"Don't forget your bike helmet," Mom shouts as she puts her shoes on out in the hall.

I read the message eight times. Then I brush my teeth and hair, make a ponytail, and look at myself in the mirror. Then I read the message five more times. I can't decide whether the short text sounds friendly or rude. *What happened to the tropics?* I don't know what to answer. I could lie and say that Mom got sick, or that the flight got canceled because of a storm. But that would just be even more lies. Even more things to keep track of.

So I don't answer.

I don't want to get to know Wilmer. I don't want to admit I lied. I can't come up with a single thing I would want to do with him. He seems kind of exhausting and lame, not my type at all. I can't imagine we'd have anything to talk about.

I decide to dare to open the window overlooking the gas station. I need air if I'm going to think clearly, and I *have* to do that now.

It seems like he wants to hang out with me since he's been throwing pebbles at my window *and* gone to the trouble of finding out what my mom's name is, calling her, asking for my number, and sending me a weird message. I'm almost impressed by the effort. I shut the window again. Maybe I can hang out with him a little bit if it's just in the backyard and no one can see us. I don't have anyone else to hang out with anyway. *And* it's been nine days since I was last outside.

That same evening, a light comes on again in Wilmer and his broke dad's apartment. I don't know if he has any siblings or a mom who's also broke or a pet. I realize I don't know anything about him, apart from the fact that he's shouting my name yet again out in the backyard. He's throwing pebbles again, too. I sit quietly and count the taps against the window each time a pebble hits. There are a lot of taps to count. I can feel the muscles in my cheeks, and how they're pulling the skin around my mouth upward—I'm actually smiling.

When the tapping finally stops, I get up and go over to the window. I breathe against the fabric of the curtains. Then I pull them open.

He's standing in the backyard, still as a statue. I'm standing totally still, too. I can hear my heart. He looks at me. I look at him. I don't think I'm smiling. He's wearing a blue T-shirt and his hair looks messy. He's not smiling, either. The seconds pass. I don't manage to count them. I just stand there. Exposed and motionless. Without a curtain to hide behind.

Then I raise my left hand, like a policeman directing traffic. Wilmer raises his right. He looks like a soldier at attention in front of a general. A little laugh escapes my lips. I can see that Wilmer is smiling. He starts waving with one arm, then the other. He hops up and down, squirming around. It looks comical. A strange, clumsy dance, like a windup toy.

Wilmer might be the world's most annoying neighbor, but if you're going to be trapped in your own house for a while, you can't be too picky. Besides, he looks *really* lame and *really* funny, dancing out there on the asphalt in the world's ugliest backyard. I fish out my phone from my pocket. I find the message from the unknown number, from the boy who's still dancing around in the summer night. And then I send a message. *No tropics*, I write, and look out the window. He stops the dancing and takes out his phone. He looks up at me.

And then there's a sound.

Meet up tomorrow? it says on my screen.

Wilmer is standing right outside the door when I go out to the backyard the next day.

"There you are," he says enthusiastically, like he's spent the first ten days of vacation standing there waiting for me specifically.

He's wearing the same shorts as the last day of school—the ones that sag in such an uncool way—and a faded black T-shirt that's way too big, with a picture of four men with long hair and a skull.

"Yeah, it's my dad's," Wilmer explains when he sees me staring at his chest. "He's kind of a metalhead."

I nod. As if that information were at all illuminating. It doesn't really seem like Wilmer cares about his choice of T-shirt. Zoo or heavy metal, it's all pretty much the same. I suddenly think about Marcus, who's always wearing nice clothes. The *complete* opposite of the boy standing in front of me.

"Sorry I've been throwing so many pebbles," Wilmer says. "I don't really know what got into me."

He shrugs.

"I'm not like one of those crazy neighbors, I mean."

He grimaces. It seems like he's trying to make himself look scary.

"I was just kind of bored."

The sun is shining on his hair and his curls glint in the light. I haven't even said a word yet. I don't know what to say. Why did I answer that message? Why did I open the curtains? Am I really *that* desperate for a friend? I suddenly regret that I didn't just stay inside the hot apartment. That was boring but uncomplicated. Now I don't know what's in store for me.

Wilmer looks toward the sandbox, the clotheslines, the rickety playset. Then he looks at me. His face lights up, and his eyes are bright blue.

"Come on. I want to show you something."

I follow Wilmer through the backyard. A man and a woman are squabbling, and a little boy has fallen off his tricycle and started crying. Wilmer walks with quick, determined steps. The end of the backyard is shady. The sun doesn't reach over the roofs here. It smells like cold asphalt.

"There," he says, pointing at a little stairwell I've never noticed before.

Seven or eight stairs go down and end at a door you

might not even see if you didn't already know about it. There are rotting leaves on the bottom step, and someone's tagged the walls.

Wilmer goes first.

"Come on, Nora," he says.

It sounds so strange when he says my name, like we're best friends going to do something fun together.

He stands outside the door and waits for me to come down. I take one step at a time until I reach the bottom. There isn't a lot of space here, and my arm grazes Wilmer's T-shirt. We're so close I can feel his breath and smell his hair.

Wilmer takes something out of his pocket. It's a tool, something sharp and metal. He leans toward the door and presses it into the lock. There's a clicking sound. And then the door opens.

"Welcome to my place." He smiles and lets me go in first.

The room is dark. It's hot and smells like basement—mildewy and stuffy.

There's a desk against one wall. It was probably white at some point, but now the paint is peeling off and turning yellow. The top drawer is open with some papers sticking out of it. A metal lamp is attached to one side, hanging limply across the top of the desk. An office chair you might have been able to sit on once has lost one of its wheels. Now it's leaning against the wall so it won't tip over. At the other end of the wall, there's a red couch covered in a kind of woolly fabric. There's an embroidered cushion lying on the couch, the kind old ladies like. The stuffing is coming out of the couch in a few places. In front of the couch is a low coffee table. On the floor next to the desk is a big toolbox with a rusty saw sticking out of it. There are two dark-brown wooden doors a bit further in. There must be more rooms.

I look around, standing completely still. What *is* this place?

A single narrow window is the only source of light until Wilmer turns on a ceiling light and comes into the room. His shoes make a weird noise like he's stepping on something sticky.

"I've been hanging out here a lot lately," he says. "A home away from home."

I still don't say a word. Wilmer just claimed that he wasn't a crazy neighbor, but I'm not really sure that's the truth. Why has he been hanging out in here? This dark basement apartment has to be the *actual* crap in Craplin Court. I start wondering how it looks in Wilmer's apartment if he prefers being here rather than at home. How lame is *his* vacation actually?

The dark T-shirt moves further into the apartment. He opens one door, and a small room with a toilet and a sink comes into view.

"Everything works," he says, turning on the tap.

He looks like an eager salesman who knows he's advertising something crappy.

"Look."

Now he's walking toward the other door. It creaks when he opens it. He leans into the room and turns on a light, then waves at me.

There's a kitchen counter at the far end of the room, a couple of dirty drinking glasses and a plate in the sink. A small fridge is in a corner. The stove top looks filthy, like someone made spaghetti and meatballs twenty years ago and forgot to clean up.

"I make food here," Wilmer says proudly.

There are two nearly empty pizza boxes on the counter—double pepperoni. He likes the same pizza I do. There's a small table and two chairs in the middle of the room. Does he eat here all by himself?

"His name was Anton," Wilmer says all of a sudden. "Anton Berntzen. The guy who lived here before."

He scratches his curls.

"I'm doing some research now," he continues. "Checking out old papers and that kind of thing. I found out he was the caretaker here in Chaplin."

He looks at me.

"But I have a sneaking suspicion that he was a pretty bad caretaker," he laughs, walking over to the fridge.

"Have a seat on the couch if you want," he says, pointing toward the living room.

The couch is surprisingly soft and comfortable. I can hear Wilmer rummaging around in the kitchen. Wilmer, who's supposed to be my friend now, I guess. Luckily there's no one around who can see me.

He pops up in the doorway a few moments later holding a tray and balancing two glasses and a bottle of soda. He's put straws in each of the glasses—one yellow and one pink.

"Ta-da," he says, smiling like an overly enthusiastic waiter at an empty pool bar.

Wilmer walks over to the yellow-white desk and opens the top drawer. A few pieces of paper flutter down to the floor like in a slow-motion movie. He bends over and picks them up.

"I found a ton of old papers," he says, and tugs out the whole drawer, bringing it over to the couch to show me.

"Most of them are just like caretaker things. He ordered light bulbs and cleaning supplies and stuff."

He holds up another piece of paper.

"And then he forgot to pay for it."

It's a letter from the bank. "Anton Berntzen must pay this amount as soon as possible!" it reads in big, bold letters.

"I'm working through the whole pile," Wilmer says, and looks at me kind of apologetically, like he gets it that reading old caretaker papers is a pretty weird thing to spend his vacation doing.

"And under here there's a *ton* of complaints. People in Chaplin were super mad at Anton. Someone's power went out. He was supposed to fix a stair. Greta Brattberg had to go to the hospital after she was messing around in a fuse box and got a shock."

Wilmer balances the drawer in his lap and leans toward me.

"Look at this."

He points at a piece of paper and reads aloud.

"We have always been happy with caretaker Anton Berntzen, but recently we've experienced that the otherwise cheerful and dutiful caretaker has become lazy, unaccommodating, and unwilling to carry out his work. If this does not change, we will ask him to resign from his position as Chaplin Court's entrusted caretaker."

I look at Wilmer, who's raising his eyebrows.

"I guess all he did was lay on this couch and chilled," Wilmer said, laughing. "Just like me. Man, I feel kind of bad for Anton."

He goes to get some more soda from the kitchen.

Then he tells me about how he discovered this place and how he broke in.

"It looked a lot worse when I came here for the first time," he says. "Now I think I've made it pretty nice."

I think about the crazy neighbor thing again. I imagine Wilmer going to his apartment to get tools and picking the lock. Breaking in like a thief and doing whatever he wants. Putting soda in the fridge and making pizza. Cleaning up after the lazy caretaker.

"I'm just really curious," says Wilmer. "And I guess it *is* pretty boring to be at home all summer."

He looks at me. His face grows serious, like he wants

me to say something. About what happened with the tropics.

I hurry to talk about Anton again.

"How long ago was he caretaker here, then?" I ask, pulling the drawer full of papers over to my lap. I root through the pile and look for dates on the letters. 1963. 1966.

"I wonder what happened to him."

I pick up a pile and catch sight of something golden at the back of the drawer beneath some envelopes.

"Whoa," says Wilmer. "I didn't see that!"

It's a gold ring. Small and delicate, it almost looks like it could fit a child. Wilmer lifts it carefully, holding it up toward the light.

"It says something inside it," I say and hold out my hand.

Wilmer places the ring in my palm.

"Your Anton," I read. "On the day of our engagement, August 16, 1962."

We look at each other and at the gold ring.

"Anton had a girlfriend," Wilmer says, amazed. A smile spreads across his face.

"But she returned the engagement ring," I say, and watch as his smile disappears.

"Maybe that's why he stopped caring about work," Wilmer sighs. "Now I feel even sorrier for him."

We finish the soda in silence. Wilmer is wearing the engagement ring on his pinkie. I check my phone to see if Mom called. I hurry to put it back in my pocket when I see Wilmer looking at my lock-screen image. It's from the pool. At Blue Lagoon Deluxe.

"When we were at that Olivia girl's place, you said you were going to the tropics," Wilmer says all of a sudden.

My face gets hot, and I look down. I don't want to talk about that. Not now. I put my left hand under my thigh and cross my fingers.

"And that felt *so* familiar to me. . ."

My stomach is prickling. At the very top, right by my heart.

"Because I've done the exact same thing myself."

I can feel his gaze even though I'm staring straight down at the floor.

"Lied."

The word hangs in the air.

"I was in the Maldives last year," he says, laughing. "Or was it Malta? I don't really remember. And it was just as nice as that tropical vacation you were talking about."

I lift my gaze up toward Wilmer's T-shirt and further to his eyes, which are serious and kind.

"I won't tell anyone," he says, smiling with his crooked tooth.

I dream about Marcus that night. He's sitting next to me on a couch, quite close. We're drinking soda with straws. I lean against his red T-shirt, smelling the scent of sunscreen and laundry detergent. Suddenly the T-shirt is black. It's Wilmer's T-shirt. Marcus has curls and a crooked front tooth. He's holding a gold ring between his thumb and index finger and asking me to marry him. Wilmer is the one talking, Wilmer is the one I'm sitting close with on the couch . . .

Then I wake up.

My phone is lighting up on the nightstand. I recognize the number. *Would be cool if you come today, too*, it says. And three happy emojis with sunglasses.

Mom is sitting in the kitchen. She made scrambled eggs and is wearing real clothes—a white skirt and a purple blouse. It looks like she just brushed her hair. The radio is playing happy music and Mom is humming along to the melody.

"Good morning, Nora," she says when I go in. She's smiling.

I stare in shock. For other people, scrambled eggs and a fully dressed mom might be totally normal, even though it's only 7:30 in the morning. But for me it's a reason to stare. It must be going well at this class, even though she says she isn't learning anything.

"What are you doing today, sweetie?"

I look out the window. It's sunny.

"The beach," I answer quickly, and look back at Mom, who's still smiling.

"With Maria?"

"Mmm-hmm," I say, nodding.

"Won't you invite Maria over here sometime?" she asks. Again. "She can even sleep over if she wants. Maybe tomorrow?"

I look at Mom. At her bright eyes, her hopeful smile. Maybe she can handle the truth now that she seems a little happier. Mom's eyebrows are raised like she's waiting for me to answer. About whether Maria wants to spend the night. My best friend. Whom I made up last winter because Mom thought it was so sad that I didn't have any friends in my new class. How am I going to get out of this? Maria's been so nice to have. I don't want to get rid of her just yet. I don't want Mom to be sad because of me when she has so much else to be sad about.

I grab my phone and quickly tap around so it looks like I'm sending a message. Mom looks excited. Maybe she's waking up a bit by going to this class. I stand and wait with my phone in my hand and pretend I get a message back.

"Oh, no," I say aloud, trying to look sad. "Maria's sick."

"Ah, that's too bad," Mom says comfortingly. "But you can just invite her again another time. There's still a lot of summer vacation left."

Since I'm supposed to be in the tropics and don't have anyone else to hang out with, I might as well hang out with Wilmer. He's cooler than I thought, actually. Pretty funny. Really weird. But in a good way. Anyway, it's just for now, during vacation. I'm not going to hang out with him after the summer. Besides, there's no one who can see I'm hanging out with him if we just stay in Chaplin Court.

To convince everyone I'm still in the tropics, I post another picture from the beach below Blue Lagoon Deluxe. *Swimming all day*, I write, and add a heart. I comment on some of the others' pictures while I wait. Emma posted a photo series of herself in front of the ocean just as the sun is setting. She looks super-pretty in the pink light. *Gorgeous*, I write, as if we're friends. A few seconds later she comments on my beach picture. *Looks sooo nice.*

Olivia also adds a comment: *Lucky duck*. It's the first time they've commented on something I posted. I feel so light. I float down the stairs and out into the backyard.

Wilmer's sitting on the red couch when I go down. He's playing on his phone and doesn't even notice that I'm standing right next to him and looking down at his screen. His thumbs move lightning fast as he controls a character shooting down some guys in a dark basement.

"Hi," I say carefully after a while.

Wilmer jumps.

"Jesus," he says. "Now I'm dead."

He puts down his phone, turns, and smiles. What is it with him and clothes, anyway? Today he's wearing a sea-weed-colored T-shirt with the words GET A LIFE written across the chest.

"Hey, I've kind of been thinking a lot about the tropics," he says.

My chest suddenly tightens again. He said he wouldn't tell anyone that I lied. Why is he bringing it up again now? Can't we just talk about something else?

"What was it that Ms. Gundersen said again?"

"Gustavsen," I correct.

"About the tropics not being any place. Like on the map. That it's just something we say about a place where you can have fun and chill and stuff."

Wilmer looks at me eagerly.

"The tropics really just means a place you go that's warmer than where you're from, right?"

I don't say anything. I don't know where he's going with this.

"Ms. Gregersen said you can decide *yourself* where the tropics are."

He looks at me like he's made a huge discovery.

"So the tropics can be here."

"Here?" I ask.

"Yeah, in the apartment. Since it's kind of . . . hot and stuff in here. Tropical, you know?"

I think my mouth has opened a tiny bit. A muscle at the corner of my mouth is quivering.

"We can just *call* it the tropics, right? Since this is just a place where you can go to have fun and chill and stuff. At least *I* do."

I look around. In that case, this would be the lamest trip to the tropics I've ever heard of, since there isn't much Blue Lagoon Deluxe in this basement apartment.

Wilmer is still smiling. Yet again, he looks like an eager salesman advertising some crap.

"It's a win-win," he says. "Then you've been in the tropics, in a way! Then you aren't really lying, right? And I can say I went to the tropics, too. That I wasn't just at home all vacation."

Am I smiling at him? I think I might be.

"No one will find out exactly where the tropics are."

He makes quotation marks with his fingers when he says, "the tropics."

"Right?"

Now I'm not sure if I'm smiling. It's a pretty lame proposition. The lamest I've heard in a long time, actually. But I like it anyway.

"Want some soda?" he asks, and heads toward the kitchen before I even manage to say yes.

T he warmth of the sun reaches all the way down into the basement apartment, blazing through the small window by the door. The sunlight shines across the couch, where we're sitting and drinking soda.

We're talking about the tropics and what we need to do to make Anton's old caretaker's apartment as "tropical" as possible. It'll take quite a lot, to say the least. I show Wilmer the pictures on my phone. Screenshots from Blue Lagoon Deluxe that I posted on our class group. Wilmer doesn't follow me, so he won't recognize them.

"Hmm," he says, looking closely at the pools and waterslides, at the man in the chef's hat and the sunset over the beach, the parasols lined up one after the other, the turquoise sea.

He goes over to Anton's desk and gets a piece of paper, then roots around trying to find something to write with. He tugs at a locked drawer, then gives up and finds a pencil in Anton's toolbox. "What we need in the tropics," he writes at the top of the page, and puts the end of the pencil in his mouth.

"A pool," I say.

Wilmer writes it down.

"Parasols? And a beach?"

I nod.

"A spa," I say. "And a kids' club. Even though we're too big for that."

Wilmer writes it down anyway. "Kids' club for the little ones." And in parentheses, he writes "not us."

"Music?"

I nod.

"There has to be dancing on the terrace every night," I add. "In the sunset."

Wilmer writes "dancing" and "sunset" as two points. He adds "terrace," too.

"Drinks," I say. "With umbrellas."

I show him the picture of Margarita in the pool bar.

"Yes," Wilmer says eagerly. "We definitely need those."

"And we need to stay in a bungalow all the way down by the beach."

The dreams I've had, the pictures I've looked at so much . . . What am I even talking about? There isn't a single thing in the caretaker's apartment that even comes close to the tropics. But I keep going anyway.

"And the beach has to be white, with blue beach chairs."

"Is it important that they're blue?" Wilmer asks as he writes.

"Not really," I say. "But they're blue at Blue Lagoon Deluxe."

"Vacation food," Wilmer suggests. "Pizza and hamburgers and fries."

It sounds good.

"Bathing suits and towels," I say. "Straw hats."

Finally, some things that are easy to find.

"I think baseball hats look better on me, though," Wilmer says, and notes down a few more points on the list.

Wilmer's piece of paper is full when we're done.

"Where do we even start?" I ask, feeling overwhelmed by the list.

It suddenly seems completely impossible to transform this lame cellar into a tropical paradise. Where are we going to find a beach and a pool and a sunset? Where will the spa be? And the kids' club for the little ones—but not us?

Wilmer looks at me. It looks like he's thinking hard beneath all the curls. His bright eyes dart from one wall to the other, searching around the room.

"We have to start with the easiest stuff," he says.

And then we make a plan.

"T he most important thing is that we make up our minds," Wilmer says after we've been at it for a few hours.

He looks at our haul. It isn't big. I got a straw hat and he got a baseball cap. We found some toys we could put in the kids' club—a teddy bear, a pink rabbit, a puzzle, and a box of crayons. Both of us brought a bathing suit and beach towel. We haven't decided where the pool and beach will be yet, but at least *that* much is in order.

"We just have to *decide* that this is the tropics."

He looks through the desk again and fishes out a pen. Then he disappears into the kitchen and comes back with a pizza box. He flattens the box, rips off the top, folds out the sides, and sits down on the floor to write.

I look at the list, trying to search deep in my brain for ideas about how we could solve the toughest points.

"I'm going to go home to look for more stuff," I say to Wilmer.

He's still sitting on the floor with the pizza box.

At home I find a couple of tall glasses. I look in the kitchen cabinet and some drawers to see if Mom happens to have some umbrellas to put in the drinks, but no. I find Mom's old beach chair in the storage room in the hallway. She hasn't used it in a while, and now she's so busy with her class she hasn't had time to sunbathe. The cover is turquoise, which is *almost* blue.

In Mom's closet I find a dress made of thin fabric with lots of patterns. It looks like a typical dress you'd wear on a beach at sunset. There's a white dress on a hanger. I think about the women in the spa in their white uniforms.

I steal body lotion and some soap from the cabinet in the bathroom and find foot cream and a nail file in a basket. I take a bag of cotton balls, too. Isn't that the kind of thing people use in spas?

I put everything in a big paper bag and take the beach chair under my arm. I run down the stairs and out into the backyard, over the teeny, tiny patch of grass, past the clotheslines and the sandbox, across the asphalt, and down the stairs to the basement apartment.

And then I see it. Wilmer has hung up a sign. You almost can't even tell it's really a pizza box. He cut it into a circle, a perfect circle. With red pen, he wrote in big, beautiful letters:

Welcome to the Tropics.

We decide the spa has to be in the bathroom.

"Should it have a name?" Wilmer shouts from the living room as I'm arranging the beauty products on the little sink.

"What about . . . Tranquil Times?" I shout back, and hear Wilmer laugh.

He shows up with a new sign, also cut out of a pizza box. TRANQUIL TIMES SPA is written in blue pen. WHERE DREAMS COME TRUE.

"Wasn't that what it said in the pictures?"

I nod. Because that's exactly what happens at the spa at Blue Lagoon Deluxe. Dreams *do* come true.

The restaurant is located in the kitchen, of course. There's a bit of work to be done here. There is truly not a single person in the whole world who'd want to step foot in this restaurant, no matter how hungry they were. We try to wash the stove, but the brown stains won't disappear. We open the kitchen cabinets and find some plates that are now stuck together since they've been sitting there for so long. We clean everything out of the cabinet—glasses, plates, a candlestick, and a coffee mug with the logo from the Lillehammer Olympics in 1994. I fill the sink with water and start washing the dishes while Wilmer keeps searching.

"Look at this," he says behind me.

He's found a tablecloth in a drawer. It's wrinkly and has brown stripes along the folds. Wilmer tries to smooth it out without much luck. He puts the candlestick in the middle of the table like he's setting up for the evening's dinner guests.

"When we get a candle, it'll be nice," he says.

Wilmer wonders if I have another idea for a name. For the restaurant this time.

"What's it called at Blue Lagoon Deluxe?" he asks.

I smile. It's so weird to hear someone say the name out loud. For such a long time, I've just been thinking it in my head, like a dream. It feels good to be able to share it with Wilmer.

"Sunlight Taverna," I say. "Doesn't that sound nice?"

The kids' club is along one wall. We set up all the games and hang up a sign. It doesn't have its own name, it's just called KIDS' CLUB FOR THE LITTLE ONES. Wilmer draws a crocodile, a doll, a red car, and a teddy bear on the sign.

We try to make it as kid-friendly as we can with what we have. Anyway, we're too big to go to the kids' club and there won't be any kids coming here.

Mom's beach chair is propped up against another wall. As soon as we know where the beach will be, we can put it out. The straw hat and baseball cap are next to it, ready for a trip to the beach.

The pool and beach and sunset have to wait a bit. We've been working for hours. Mom will be home from her class soon, and I promised her I'd be there when she got back.

"The tropics weren't built in a day," Wilmer says as he shuts the door to the caretaker's apartment.

We walk up the little staircase from the basement and suddenly feel how hot it is outside. The sun is still high in the sky. It smells like asphalt and grilled hot dogs. There are a few people spraying each other with a garden hose on the grass, laughing and running around. Three women are sitting in deck chairs by a plastic pool where two small children are splashing around.

All of a sudden, it looks nice. Here. In Craplin Court. Or is it just me? Seeing things I don't normally see?

I walk over to Building A and turn around. I can see Wilmer opening the door to Building F. I look at his green T-shirt, at all his curls.

"Wilmer!" I shout.

He turns. There isn't really anything I actually want to say, no reason to shout. I just stand there and look at him. He waves.

Then the door slams behind him and he's gone.

have more fun in the tropics than I do with slime. I just want to keep going, gather everything we need, make it nice in the caretaker's apartment, create a tropical paradise. Sometimes I realize how childish this game really is, and how embarrassing it would be if someone knew what we were doing or if anyone saw me with Wilmer. It seems like he doesn't even care that it's childish. He just has fun and comes up with one idea after the other. I often forget that it's childish when I'm with him.

After we've eaten dinner and I've lied to Mom about how nice the water was at the beach, I get started.

I look at the photograph I took of our list and start at the top. "Pool." It's an obvious challenge. I Google around for a while and find companies that can come and dig in people's gardens. Round pools. Square. Oval. Environmentally friendly. There are pictures of happy people splashing and sunbathing at the edge of the pool. No one is lying in a pool in a basement apartment.

Suddenly I remember the inflatable pool out in the backyard. I think of what Wilmer said about how it's important to just make up your mind about things.

I look around a bit online. A plastic pool costs anywhere between ten and forty dollars, depending on what model you want. I don't have ten dollars and I don't think Wilmer does either. I don't want to ask Mom, and Wilmer's dad is broke. I go on Craigslist and look under "Free." I write "pool" in the search bar and narrow down the search so I only get results from nearby. Only one result shows up. A little pink Hello Kitty pool. In Solvang Heights!

I look up "parasol," too, and find a bright red one someone is trying to get rid of. Unfortunately, it doesn't close, the ad says.

"Sunset," I write in the search bar. Several results show up. Things that only match the word *sun*. Things that only match the word *set*. A book with the word *sunset* in the title. I scroll down, searching and searching. And then I find it: a big roll of wallpaper. It's a beautiful picture of a beach with palm trees and white sand under an incredible pink sunset.

I save all my results and send messages to the people giving things away. Then I pull up Wilmer's number. *Important things have been found*, I write. He answers about three seconds later. *Important things have been found here, too*, it says. And then a yellow thumbs-up.

Wilmer is already there when I go down to the basement the next day. I wonder when he leaves his apartment, and how long he's been sitting on the red couch playing on his phone. It really seems like he doesn't have anyone other than his dad to look after him, and it seems like he can't even manage to do that very well.

Wilmer is wearing a white T-shirt today, and for once there isn't any writing or pictures on it. It even fits him. There's a big blue IKEA bag in the middle of the floor with an electric cord sticking out of it.

"Yesss!" he says, and finishes the game. "I won!"

He looks at me inquisitively.

"Where's the stuff you found?" he asks when he sees I haven't brought anything with me.

"It's on Craigslist," I reply.

"Craigslist?"

He looks disappointed and points at the blue IKEA bag.

"Mine's here," he says, and shows me a yellow beach towel, a pack of candles, and a little speaker. He made a playlist with tropical music, he says.

"And check this out."

He pulls on the cord that's sticking out of the bag, and I can see there are light bulbs in all colors attached to it. Green, purple, blue, pink, and yellow.

"Doesn't this seem like the kind of thing you'd see on vacation in the tropics?" Wilmer asks happily.

He stands with the cord in his hand and looks around to figure out where the lights would look best.

"There?" he asks, pointing at the window.

I nod. Wilmer gets some nails out of the toolbox and hammers them into the wall. We hang the cord with the lights across the nails in an arch around the little window and almost all the way to the door.

"Did you check if they work?" I ask.

Wilmer takes the plug to the closest outlet.

"Ready, set, go!" he says, and plugs it in.

The bulbs light up—most of them, anyway. The caretaker's apartment looks like a beach bar bathed in a nice, warm light.

"Wow," I say, surprised, and my arm suddenly brushes against Wilmer's back.

He looks at me.

"Now we're talking tropical vibes, right?"

We decide to get sand out of the sandbox in the back-yard.

"If it doesn't smell like cat pee," I say.

It isn't white or tropical, but there isn't anyone giving away sand on Craigslist. I checked. We agreed that we don't need all that much anyway. We just have to *decide* that it's a beach, Wilmer says, leading me out into the backyard.

Our little sandy beach looks kind of sad when it's done. It isn't white. It isn't long. And it doesn't end in a turquoise sea. It doesn't help much to set up Mom's old beach chair, either.

We take a break on the couch and sip soda.

"I wonder if Anton Berntzen is still alive," I say, and see that Wilmer still hasn't taken off the ring. "Have you tried Googling him?"

I don't wait for an answer and pick up my phone. If there's one thing I can do, it's Google. Wilmer leans toward me to see what I'm writing. He smells like sun-screen, which is kind of weird since he's spending his vacation in a basement apartment with only one window.

I try a few variations. "Anton Berntzen + caretaker" doesn't have any results. I try "Chaplin Court + 1960s + 30 Miller Avenue." But nothing comes up.

"I checked the names on the mailboxes one day when I

didn't have anything to do," Wilmer says. "I saw that one of them was Greta Brattberg."

He looks at me.

"You know, the one who complained about the care-taker because she got shocked by the fuse box and had to go to the hospital."

I laugh.

"I think she still lives here."

"We can check," I say eagerly. "Maybe she knows what happened to Anton Berntzen."

ritten on the door is "G. Brattberg." She lives on the third floor in Building H. It smells sweet in the hallway, and Wilmer says he thinks it must be pancakes.

He knocks on her door, and we wait patiently. We hear some noises from inside the apartment, some shuffling coming closer and closer. The door finally opens and a face appears in a narrow crack.

"What is it?"

She has a security lock on the door, a thick chain that splits her face in two as she stands there staring at us.

"We live here in Chaplin," Wilmer says. "And we'd like to speak with you."

"I'm not buying any raffle tickets!" Greta Brattberg says firmly. "You won't sell so much as a ball of yarn to me!"

I smile at the face in the door.

"We want to talk to you about the old days," I say.

She looks a bit surprised and shuts the door. We hear

a clicking noise and then she opens the door wide, and the sweet scent of what must be pancakes hits us.

"I love talking about the old days," says Greta Brattberg. Her face radiates like someone's suddenly flipped on a light switch. "Come in."

We walk into a hallway that's exactly the same as the one we have at home. Greta Brattberg is shorter than Wilmer and thinner than me. Her eyes are brown and lively, her hair gathered in a bun on top of her head.

"Don't mind my mess," she says, pointing into the living room where newspapers are scattered all over the floor. The windows are covered with heavy dark-blue curtains. A black cat creeps around the couch.

"His name is Henry," says Greta Brattberg. "It's not really a cat's name, but I couldn't come up with anything better."

Wilmer bends over to pet Henry. I look at Greta.

"What do you want to know about the old days?" she asks eagerly, waving her hands to signal that we should sit down.

We hesitate a bit as if neither of us can manage to start with the most important things.

"Have you lived here long?" I ask, and Greta nods.

"Born and raised in Chaplin."

"We were wondering if you remember a caretaker? His name was Anton Berntzen. It was probably a while ago now."

Greta looks at us.

"Do you want waffles?" she asks suddenly, and stands up before we manage to answer.

She goes out into the kitchen and rattles around some plates.

"Waffles," Wilmer says, and smiles at me. "Those smell just like pancakes, right?"

Greta comes back with a tower of waffles.

"Anton Berntzen," she says, and passes us some jam, "was the greatest caretaker of all time. He could do everything a caretaker should. And not just that, he was kind. Intelligent. Charming. *And* he played the accordion."

She pours syrup onto a waffle, smiling as she eats it.

"Do you know where he lives now?" I ask.

Greta looks at us gravely.

"In heaven, I hope," she says quietly.

"So he's dead?"

She nods.

"He was just a shadow of himself for the last few years. He mostly stayed in his apartment and read. I think he liked poetry."

She folds a waffle in two and gobbles it down as she keeps talking.

"I remember when he got together with the pretty girl. That's what we called her. *The pretty girl.* I can't remember what her name was. Something having to do with birds?"

Wilmer looks at me and puts his hand with the ring on his knee.

"And Anton was so in love. He strutted around Chaplin to show her off. She was tall and slim, and he was short and fat. They were quite the pair."

"But what happened?" Wilmer asks impatiently after Greta's been quiet for a few seconds.

She takes a deep breath.

"Paris," she says. "I heard that was where she went. At least, she got a job as a model. That's what happens when you're so pretty. And then it was over and out with Anton."

Wilmer strokes the ring that might have belonged to a Parisian model.

"I think he was heartbroken for the rest of his life."

Greta Brattberg looks at me, then at Wilmer.

"You young ones probably don't really know what it is to be in love," she says. "But it can be quite scary."

Wilmer giggles a bit, and Greta's eyes widen.

"Are you in love with someone?" she asks suddenly. "Be honest."

Something tightens in my stomach, or in my heart. Yes, it must be in my heart. I don't dare look at Wilmer or at his face. I look down at the nice boy's hands that are sitting in his lap. The index finger of his right hand is tapping restlessly against his knee.

"I don't think so," he says.

He's speaking very quietly. I can barely hear the four words, even though he's sitting so close I can almost feel his breath against my cheek. His face is bright red and he squirms in his chair.

"But the day you do fall in love," Greta Brattberg says, holding up a finger in front of Wilmer, "you need to be careful. Love can be dangerous."

Wilmer nods. Some of his curls are sticking to his forehead. He doesn't look at me. But I'm looking at him. At his chest, like I'm trying to look straight into his heart and figure out how it's put together.

We're already on our way to pick up the little pool when I suddenly realize that I'm *actually* still supposed to be in the tropics. I posted a picture from Blue Lagoon Deluxe only last night and wrote that it was super hot. Even Marcus liked the picture. What if I see someone from my class while I'm walking with Wilmer? How am I going to explain that?

Wilmer is walking quietly beside me. I really want him to be impressed by my effort. Everything I've managed to Google. What if he thinks an inflatable Hello Kitty pool is lame or the wallpaper with the sunset or the red parasol that doesn't close?

We call the people who are giving away the pool. Their house looks like the one Olivia lives in—big and white, like most of the houses in this neighborhood. The woman who opens the door looks at us a bit strangely.

"My mom told me that I'm supposed to pick up a Hello Kitty pool," I say as sweetly as I possibly can. "It's for my little sister."

The woman in the door smiles.

"It's out in the carport," she says, pointing toward a building where the back of a huge car is sticking out.

We get what looks like a plastic bag out of the garage. I pull at the plastic and try to unfold it so Wilmer can see what our new pool will look like.

"Genius," he says. "Now we can cross the pool off our list."

I can tell Wilmer is impressed with the wallpaper, too. We roll it out carefully on the sidewalk so he can see how nice the sunset is going to look in the tropics. *Our* tropics. How white the sand is, how the palm tree is kind of blowing in the evening breeze. We decide that it has to hang on the wall by the lights.

"It's going to be so cool," Wilmer says.

And then his arm brushes against mine and I can feel his warm skin.

Next on our list is the parasol. We have to walk pretty far to get it. Wilmer carries the roll of wallpaper and I carry the little pool. We walk so long that the sun disappears behind a cloud and it gets chilly. A flock of birds takes off from a tree like they're already heading south for winter.

"Is that it?" Wilmer asks, pointing.

A red parasol is lying like an upturned toadstool in a garage. I check the address and nod.

"It doesn't fold up," I explain. "So we just have to carry it like this."

We walk home beneath the red parasol. People look at us and smile. We smile back and say hi to everyone we see. Wilmer's face gets such a nice color with the red from the parasol reflected on his face. He looks tan, almost a little sunburned.

We're halfway home to the tropics when we hear it—a thunderclap. A *really* powerful one. And then it starts raining. First, only a few drops hit the parasol, making a light pitter-patter. Then it gets more and more powerful until it's drumming against the red roof. We crouch beneath the parasol. Close together. Wilmer holds tightly to the roll of wallpaper so the sunset won't fall apart. My canvas shoes get wet and my feet are cold. It thunders and rumbles. Lightning flashes. We count. One thousand and one. One thousand and two. One thousand and three. We look at each other when the thunder really starts booming, like someone is splitting the sky in two with a chain saw.

"Are you scared of thunderstorms?" Wilmer asks.

"No," I lie.

We stand close beneath the red roof until the worst has passed, both holding onto the parasol. Wilmer puts his hand over mine. I don't dare look at him. My chest thuds like part of the thunderstorm has rumbled into my body. You probably can't even see my face anymore since it's as red as the parasol. The water splashes and cascades along the sidewalk. The parasol gets heavier. And Wilmer's face is very close. His lips, his eyes, his hair.

Then it's quiet. Wilmer sticks his head out from under the parasol.

We keep walking. Home to the tropics.

We work for the rest of the day, blowing up the little pool, filling it with water, deciding where the pool area should be, and putting our bathing suits and towels on a chair next to it. We set out some glasses with hot-pink umbrellas. The pool bar, as Wilmer calls it.

The wallpaper should really be attached with glue, but Anton doesn't have any in his toolbox. We have to use thumbtacks, which is pretty hard. We each stand on a chair and work our way toward the middle. We fasten the wallpaper all the way by the ceiling and pull it down the wall so it won't curl up. Then we take a few steps back to admire the sunset behind the colorful lights.

"This is seriously the nicest sunset I've ever seen," Wilmer says dreamily.

The parasol is so wet we don't want to take it inside to the beach, so we leave it on the stairs by the basement to dry off. We look at the list of tropical things and realize most of it's checked off.

"What do we . . . do now?" I ask Wilmer.

Wilmer looks at me in surprise, like he thinks my question is one of the silliest he's ever heard.

"We have fun in the tropics!" he says.

And smiles.

I go to the tropics as soon as Mom leaves for her class. Every morning, I run through the backyard, and as soon as I see the sign that says WELCOME TO THE TROPICS, my heart starts beating like a drum.

Every day, Wilmer is sitting on the red couch playing on his phone, and every day he looks just as happy when I interrupt his game, even though it always ends with him dying. We usually sit next to each other on the couch and chat for a bit before we decide what we're going to do. And then we do tropical things.

We swim in the pool. It's so small there's only room for one of us at a time, and even then you can barely crouch down in the water if you fold your body in half. The other person usually hangs out at the pool bar in the meantime, with soda and an umbrella in a tall glass. Then we switch.

We eat at Sunlight Taverna—pizza or hot dogs since that's easiest to make. Sometimes, if we don't have any money to buy anything, we just eat sandwiches, but then we call them *club* sandwiches. Wilmer lights a candle and plays waiter.

"Was it a latte you were having?" he asks courteously, holding out the Olympics mug.

I go to Paradise Spa and get a facial from Wilmer. He puts on Mom's white dress and downloads some relaxing music—pan flutes and violins.

"Relax, relax," he says in a high voice, and then he dips some cotton balls in water and strokes them carefully over my face.

Neither of us suggests dancing in the sunset, even though it's a typical tropical thing we talked about doing. Dancing would just be way too embarrassing, whether we're dancing by ourselves or together. We listen to the playlist and sit on the red couch with the view of the sunset. But we don't dance.

We're not at the beach that much either since it's pretty lame, but sometimes we pretend we're sunbathing, just to say we've done it. I sit on Mom's beach chair and Wilmer on his beach towel. We have to shut our eyes because of the blazing sun, and sometimes we fall asleep. At least I do.

"Have you ever actually been to the tropics, Nora?" Wilmer asks one day when we're lying there.

"No," I say. "Have you?"

"Yeah," he says. "Once."

I turn over on my side and look at him. He puts his hands behind his head and they disappear in his curls. His T-shirt is light blue and advertising Best Buy.

"But I like this tropical trip a lot more," he says, and squints up at me with one eye like he's actually lying on a beach in the sun.

"Really?" I ask.

"Yeah."

He doesn't say anything for a while. He shuts his eyes again.

"Since no one here is drunk."

I stand by the window at night before I go to sleep and look over at Building F, at his window on the third floor. Sometimes he waves to me from his room. I wave back, put my arms under my chin like I'm sleeping on them, and then give him a thumbs-up. To say that he should sleep well.

I often think about Wilmer when I'm going to sleep. I dream about him, too. He's always wearing a red T-shirt in the dream. It's kind of weird that it's red since I've never actually seen Wilmer in that color.

We've talked about what will happen to the tropics when summer vacation is over. Should we pack everything up, now that everything looks so nice?

"People *do* go to the tropics in the fall, too," Wilmer says, and looks at me.

I don't say anything about what I'd thought before we started doing all of this—that Wilmer is just someone I hang out with because there isn't anyone else, that we're not going to be friends when summer is over, that there probably won't be any trips to the tropics in the fall.

We decided that everything that is said in the tropics stays in the tropics. Like a kind of pact. A secret agreement. Maybe that's why it's so easy to talk to each other? I talk about Mom being tired all the time and that lame class she's taking. About how we don't have much money. About how we've moved so many times that the number of friends I have is just about zero. I talk about all the things I've lied about. The beach and Maria, Olivia's present, the pictures I've been posting of my vacation from Blue Lagoon Deluxe. Wilmer sits on the red couch and listens. It doesn't seem like he thinks I'm stupid.

Then he talks about himself, too—about why they moved here, about his dad who's nice and pretty funny but likes beer a little too much. About his mom who moved to Sweden and had kids with a guy named Sven. She calls every Tuesday and Friday on FaceTime.

It's weird with Wilmer, who's really just supposed to be a summer friend. Suddenly I don't understand anything anymore. I don't want to think. I just want to stay in the tropics. I just want to sit in the beach chair, eat at the Taverna, look at the sunset. With him. Wilmer feels like a friend. Maybe a best friend. Maybe more.

've lost track of how many days of vacation have passed. I've stopped counting hours. Minutes. Seconds. The best part of the day is when I go into the tropics and see Wilmer on the couch. When he turns and smiles at me.

But today, he isn't sitting there. I can see his back over by the desk. He's tugging and pulling at the locked drawer, standing there with a tool in one hand, a kind of rod that's bent at one end.

"Hi," he says, turning and smiling.

He's wearing the T-shirt from the zoo again, the one he was wearing the very first time I saw him. I thought it was ugly then. Now I kind of like the green color.

"I *will* get this drawer open today," he says breathlessly, showing me the tool. "But I've given up on finding the key."

He puts the end of the rod in the edge of the drawer and tugs. The wood creaks and part of the drawer comes off. I walk over to him and hold onto the tool, too, pushing and pressing with Wilmer. Suddenly the drawer loosens, and we fall backward with a jerk.

The drawer is almost empty. Wilmer looks sad. He picks up an envelope and a red book.

We take the modest haul over to the couch. The envelope is open, and the address has been scribbled over with a thick pen. Wilmer pulls the letter out eagerly and unfolds a piece of paper with a few sentences. The writing is crooked.

"Dear Frida," Wilmer reads. "I saw your picture and read about you in the newspaper. It's nice that you're doing so well. Things are mostly good here at home. I . . ."

The rest of the short text is scribbled over. Wilmer turns the paper, reading the words that are possible to decipher.

Think about you. A lot. Love. Far too much. Every single day. Regret. Home again. Dearest.

"It's a love letter!"

I look at Wilmer, at his pretty eyes, his hair.

"But he never sent it," he says, holding out the envelope. "There's no stamp here."

I pick up the red book. It makes a crackly noise when I open it. A piece of paper is sticking out from the middle. It's a newspaper photograph. The woman in the picture has dark shoulder-length hair, brown eyes, and a mole on one cheek. It looks like it was taken by a professional photographer. She smiles with straight, white teeth.

"*The pretty girl!*" Wilmer whispers and looks at me. "Frida."

The red book is full of poems that Anton wrote. Some are about sunsets and birds and waves in the sea, but most of them are about Frida.

We read some of the poems aloud to each other. It's embarrassing, both because they're bad and because they're about love. We try not to laugh—after all, it was Anton who wrote this, and if there's anyone we feel sorry for, it's him. But sometimes it's hard not to. Anton compares Frida to a stew full of heavenly ingredients—exciting, supple, and tasty. He says she's as interesting as a toolbox.

"Good thing he was a caretaker, I guess," Wilmer mumbles.

We hang the picture of Frida on the wall, standing there for a long time looking at her pretty face smiling in our tropical paradise.

"I understand why Anton was in love with her," Wilmer says, and looks at me.

I feel my face getting warm, red, the prickling on my cheeks.

"Imagine if they sat here," he continues dreamily, "on the red couch, right where we always sit. And were in love. Kissing and stuff. Imagine that, Nora."

Wilmer looks at me. His cheeks are a little red, too. I hurry to find my phone.

"I wonder if Frida's still alive," I say, and start typing frantically.

It's good to have something to do now that I'm so red and embarrassed. I open Google and look up "frida + model + paris." Nothing shows up. I try "engagement + 1962 + frida + anton berntzen," but nothing leads us any further.

"If we only knew her last name," I say.

We just stand there looking at the pretty one on the wall. Frida without the last name. Anton's great love.

"You remember the thing with the bungalow?" Wilmer asks as I'm getting ready to leave.

It suddenly seems like he doesn't want me to go since he stops me by the door.

"We kind of forgot about that. There was supposed to be a bungalow here."

I nod. I hadn't thought about the bungalow at all, not for a long time.

"I mean, maybe we could sleep over here one night," he says.

He looks at me inquisitively.

"We could try spending the night. If you wanted to, I mean. But then we'd probably need a bungalow."

It isn't possible to stuff a bungalow in here now, or ever.

"We can sleep on the couch," I say.

I think of Mom right away. I can't tell her I'm going to sleep in a caretaker's basement apartment. She'd freak out.

"And maybe one of us can sleep on a camping mattress on the floor," I continue, as if I've already forgotten about the thing with Mom.

"Yeah," Wilmer says eagerly. "I can take the mattress and you can take the couch."

He looks at me.

"Maybe tomorrow?"

"Maybe," I reply.

Something is different. I can feel it in my chest, right beneath my heart. Or maybe *in* it.

What is it about Wilmer? I want to touch his T-shirt, sit next to him on the red couch—*close*. I want to hear his voice and his laughter, to look at his back when he goes to Sunlight Taverna to get soda for me.

Mom calls out that the food is almost ready. I say that I'm coming but keep lying there, thinking. My cheeks are prickling, and a warm wave washes over my body.

The world's most irritating neighbor. I want to stroke the skin on his arm and put my hand in his the way couples do.

Oh my God. I get up abruptly from my bed. Wilmer is a friend I *really* don't need. I need friends who lift me up, not pull me down. And Wilmer is *never* going to be the right kind of guy. Popular, like Marcus. He's too weird, he wears lame T-shirts, and he doesn't have any social skills. He just says whatever he wants and doesn't care about what people think of him. I was only supposed to hang out with Wilmer over the summer since I didn't have anyone else to hang out with. He was just supposed to be a vacation friend. Someone you forget when summer is over. That was how it was supposed to be.

Mom has lit candles and put out a tablecloth. There are even some flowers in a vase.

"Well," she says, pouring juice into my glass. "This isn't exactly a dream summer, but we're making the most of it."

I don't say anything. Dream summer. I was very determined about what a *dream summer* meant before vacation started, but now I've changed my mind.

"But you've been so good at entertaining yourself," Mom says. "Grandma says so, too. You never make any trouble, and I'm so proud of that."

She takes the pizza cutter and rolls it back and forth forcefully. She picks up a piece and puts it on my plate, a long string of cheese trailing behind it.

"By the way, Nora," Mom says when she sits down. "There's a woman in my class who invited me over tomorrow night."

She smiles uncertainly.

"To have some wine. But I don't really know. It could get late. She invited me over at eight."

Mom looks like a seven-year-old who wants birthday

cake on a Wednesday. Like *I'm* suddenly the grown-up here.

It takes about ten seconds before I understand what she's saying. When I've gotten over the shock that Mom has made a friend *and* that she's been invited somewhere and actually looks happy for once, I understand the opportunities I have in front of me.

"I think you should go," I say, trying not to look too eager. "It sounds fun."

"It does, doesn't it?" Mom says. "She's very nice. Her name is Jane. But she lives pretty far away."

Mom hasn't changed into sweatpants. She's sitting at the table in normal clothes. Pretty nice clothes, even—a white blouse and blue pants and big silver earrings. She's still smiling at me uncertainly when I make my final move.

"Could I sleep over at Maria's, then?" I ask, thinking of Wilmer. "She just asked and it would be a great time to have a sleepover."

Mom's face lights up.

"Yes, of course," she says brightly. "That's totally fine with me. That's great, Nora!"

"Perfect," I say. "Then you don't have to think about me, at least."

Mom laughs and puts her hand over mine on the table. "But I'm always thinking about you, sweetie."

I can't believe how well that went! I lie on my bed with my phone and wonder how I'm going to tell Wilmer. I try different things: *I can do it tomorrow. Sleepover it is. Mom said yes.* But I delete them all as soon as I've written them. I end up sending a thumbs-up and the word *bungalow.*

Mom gave me some money. That almost never happens, but now I have ten dollars I can use to buy something for me and Maria. She's *that* happy to be able to drink wine at Jane's.

I go to the store and buy candy and Cheetos. Wilmer said he'll get some more pizza. He bought soda, too, so soon we'll have everything we need.

I don't dare take my duvet. It would seem weird if Maria doesn't have extra blankets, and Mom will come home later and see that my duvet is missing. I text Wilmer and ask if he can take an extra one for me.

As soon as I walk through the backyard, everything feels different—in the very best way. It makes my head spin a little. It isn't just a regular day in the tropics, I guess. The playset, the clotheslines, the little grassy area, the yellow brick buildings . . . Everything that's *actually* ugly suddenly seems nice today. Craplin Court has transformed.

I stop outside the door and smile at the sign. It's different. Wilmer wrote another line. FRIDA AND ANTON'S PARADISE, it says in blue marker.

As always, Wilmer is sitting on the red couch, and as always, he's in the middle of a game. He types like a madman and it almost looks like he's trying to destroy his phone with aggressive fingers. He's wearing a red T-shirt today. What is it that's so special about that? Why do I turn red myself, just because he happens to be wearing a red T-shirt?

"Hi," I say, even though I know Wilmer doesn't like to be startled.

He keeps playing, but then it comes:

"Ugh, I'm dead."

He turns and smiles. I don't really know what to say, so I don't say anything. I just stand there and look stupidly at my tropical friend with the red T-shirt and curls going in all different directions. I smile back. Then I realize I usually sit down next to him, so I do. We just sit there on the couch for a while without talking. And he looks really good in red.

It seems like Wilmer's different today, too. He doesn't say anything to me at first. Then he starts talking a *lot*. About anything and everything possible. But then he goes quiet again. He looks the other way every time I look at him.

We do all the tropical things we usually do—heat up piz-za and eat at Sunlight Taverna. Stuff our mouths full of Cheetos even though we're already super full. Wilmer lies on his beach towel and I sit in the beach chair. I think we've both almost fallen asleep, or at least I'm so out of it that at first I don't really understand where the sound is coming from. Suddenly I hear buzzing and beeping, and I sit up.

My phone is lighting up on the floor right next to the beach. I can see there's a message on the display, so I lean over and pick it up.

It's from Olivia! She's never sent a message just to me before.

Was just wondering if you're still having fun in the tropics? She added a winking smiley face.

"Look at this," I say to Wilmer, surprised.

He gets up from the towel and comes over, leaning forward to see what it says. His curls tickle my cheek.

"So weird," he says. "Are you guys friends, then?"

I shake my head.

"She doesn't like me at all. We're like the opposite of friends."

It's weird now with Olivia and Emma and Marcus and all of them. Normally they're so important. Normally I think about them all the time. I'm so scared of them, but I still want to be friends with them. I've forgotten all about them recently, but now it's like they're suddenly showing up again, and the same old feelings come back.

I sit there for a few seconds, wondering how I should respond. How long did I say I was going to be in the tropics? It was only two days ago that I posted the picture of the chef in the tall hat in front of the enormous buffet and wrote that I had everything I could ever want. Marcus liked it. Olivia and Emma, too. I can really only say yes, that I'm having fun. I don't need to go into detail, and besides, I really *am* in the tropics. It's just different from what Olivia would expect.

Before I manage to think any more, I've pressed send. *Yeah*, is all I write in the message. And then a regular smiley face that isn't winking.

It's only about five seconds before there's another beep.

Send a picture then, it says. *Of yourself!* No smiley face this time.

"What do I do now?" I ask meekly.

Wilmer looks at me.

"Give me your phone," he says firmly.

I reluctantly hand him my phone. I don't want him to do anything crazy. He doesn't understand how important all of this with Olivia and Emma is. He doesn't care.

"Go over there," he says.

"Here?" I ask, moving toward the sunset.

Wilmer holds out the phone, staring at the screen.

"Perfect," he says. "But you have to put on some other clothes."

I suddenly understand what Wilmer means and pick up my bathing suit that's lying over by the little Hello Kitty pool. I go into the spa and change, then stand in front of the sunset again.

"It totally looks real," Wilmer says, snapping away. "They aren't even going to realize it's fake."

We send two pictures from the white beach in the sunset, with me smiling in my bathing suit in front of the palms that are blowing a bit in the breeze. *Blue Lagoon Deluxe is paradise*, I write.

Then I hurry to put my phone on silent before Olivia has time to reply.

I t is a nice, warm summer evening. A dream summer evening. We have to open the little window to let some air in. We open the door, too, and sit on the stairs a bit, leaning against the warm brick wall. I think about Mom drinking wine at Jane's. She must be having fun. Maybe she's even on her way to becoming a Mom who can actually do things.

It's still and muggy. Maybe a thunderstorm is on its way. I look at Wilmer in his red T-shirt. I feel happy. Our knees bump together. His warm skin against mine.

What's so great about Wilmer is that we can just sit like this. Completely silent, without it being awkward at all. And then we can just start talking again, which Wilmer does after we've been sitting on the stairs for a while, our knees touching.

"How much of summer vacation is left, actually?" he asks.

I normally have a complete grasp of hours and minutes and seconds, but now I have no idea how long it is until school starts again.

"I feel like summer's gone by insanely fast," he continues when he realizes I don't have an answer to his question.

"Me too," I say, and think about the day Mom told me about her class. Then, I thought I'd be sitting inside, bored out of my mind every single day for the entire summer. It's so different now, though. All because of Wilmer.

We go back in when it gets late and listen to music from Wilmer's playlist. All of a sudden, he jumps up from the couch and walks into the middle of the floor, starting to move in front of the sunset. From side to side. With strange, slow movements to the music. Is that . . . dancing?

"It *is* on the list," he says when he sees me laughing.

And then he stretches out an arm as though he wants me to dance with him. In front of the wallpaper with the sunset.

What's so great about Wilmer is that we can dance in the sunset without it being awkward. We joke around and laugh, moving awkwardly and clumsily, singing at the top of our lungs. Wilmer tries to do the splits. I try to do ballet, pirouetting across the floor. We jump around and go totally crazy.

Until the slow song. The one about love and the heart and pain.

"Now I think we have to do this," Wilmer says, holding out his arms.

I walk toward him and he catches me like an octopus. He puts his arms around my waist and I put my arms on his shoulders, and we're so close that my heart starts pounding again. And then we dance like grown-ups dance, slowly from side to side. Without either of us talking or joking around. Wilmer's arms are nice and warm. Everything is nice and warm.

We brush our teeth in Paradise Spa before we go to bed. Wilmer brought duvets but forgot a mattress, so we decide that we can both sleep on the couch.

We lie quietly on our own side of the couch, our feet at opposite ends. It's almost dark in the room; only a faint strip of light comes in from the little window and splits the tropics in two.

"Wilmer," I say.

"Yeah?"

"Are you asleep?"

It's so stupid to ask someone who's just said "yeah" if he's sleeping.

"What is it?" he asks, turning over.

I think. About what I want to ask him. What I'm afraid of asking him.

"When we were at Greta Brattberg's," I stammer, and

take a long pause. "You said you didn't have a crush on anyone."

It's quiet.

"Yeah?" Wilmer says after way too many seconds.

I sit up to look at him. It feels weird to talk about such serious things when you're lying head to feet on a couch. Wilmer is lying on his side. His face is buried in the cushion and I can barely see it.

I don't manage to continue. I don't have any words prepared in my head. Nothing useful, at least. A few seconds pass. I would've counted if I were my usual self, but I'm not. I haven't been myself in a long time.

"I think that might have been a lie."

He's still lying in the same position. His eyes are shut and it's almost like he's talking in his sleep.

"What do you mean?" I ask softly.

Wilmer puts his arm over his face so it's even harder to see him.

"It was a lie," he says.

I swallow. What does that really mean? I bump his feet so he'll react. He has to explain what he means. I can't stand riddles. I *hate* riddles. At least about such important things.

"I think I do now."

He sits up on the couch and looks at me. His eyes are kind and round, like a faithful dog's. There's a pounding in my heart, not my stomach.

It's nice and quiet in the tropics. He takes his hand off the duvet and puts it on mine. Our fingers intertwine. He doesn't ask if I have a crush on anyone because I guess it's obvious. Maybe he can see it on the skin over my heart, or the redness of my face, or my lips that can't do anything but smile.

"You're so pretty," Wilmer whispers.

I get as red as all the red T-shirts in the world.

He moves. We sit close together without saying anything, just breathing. He puts his head on my shoulder. His curls tickle my chin. And then it happens. In one big movement. We kiss. We hold each other. His breath is warm against my cheek, his lips soft. He smells like Wilmer. He smells good.

We sleep next to each other on the couch, Wilmer's breath in my ear, his hand against my back. I think about everything possible before I manage to fall asleep. Kissing. Dancing in the sunset. The picture I sent to Olivia. Mom at Jane's. Maria, whom I'm supposed to be having a sleepover with. The dream summer. And what's going to happen when vacation is over.

ilmer isn't on the couch when I wake up the next day. It's cold in the room, and I can hear rain falling outside. I stretch and take note of my body. It's like everything's been put together in a new way. My muscles and joints. My skin. My hair and nails. I touch my lips. They're rough. They're cracked in a couple of places so some of the skin has come loose. *Is it because of the kissing?* I think and feel a tingling all the way down to my toes just from the thought. It's just like something is loosening in my stomach and throbbing against my guts. My heart pounds so hard I have to turn on my side. My body is sore after having slept huddled together, two bodies on one couch.

Where is he, actually? I sit up on the couch, and then I hear it. He's clattering around in Sunlight Taverna. Something smells good.

I pick up my phone from the floor and turn off "do not disturb."

And then I see it.

Someone has called me. Twelve times. What happened? I tap on the green phone icon. Olivia! She tried to call me twelve times! My stomach pounds. My lips feel even drier. My muscles tense up. Why in the world has Olivia called me so many times? She's never called me before.

I tap back to the home screen and see the number seven over the message inbox. I hesitate for a few seconds before I tap on it.

We're heading over to your house now. Just so you know.

I get up and stand there with my phone in my hand, holding it like it's a weapon, something dangerous. I mostly want to throw it. Let it explode like a grenade over by the wall so I won't get hurt as badly. But it just lies heavily in my hand. I can't throw it. They're coming over here. What is happening?

I scroll back through the messages. I can't even read everything, I just see words that pop out of Olivia's message bubbles. *We know everything. Liar.* I work my way backward, all the way to the picture I sent to Olivia yesterday. My chest prickles when I see it—myself in a bathing suit in front of the sunset. Our sunset. Wilmer's and mine. It suddenly looks so lame. *I* suddenly look so lame. So pathetic in the childish bathing suit in front of the fake sunset that's really just wallpaper. Suddenly I'm Nora, the old Nora. Everything comes back. Suddenly

I'm scared again. Scared of Olivia and Emma and Marcus, of the groups in the playground. Of birthdays and vacations and everything I have to lie about and pretend to do. Everything they can find out...if they just look properly.

We know you aren't in the tropics!

I stare at the first message. It was sent right after I turned off my phone, right after the picture of the sunset.

Why are you lying?

My eyes sting and throb. My throat tightens, my head feels hot and fuzzy.

Emma and I went to your place to get the birthday present you forgot to give me. And your mom said you were sleeping over at Maria's!

I blink quickly before I read on.

Your best friend Maria who's in our class! HAHAHA.

My heart. It's never pounded so fast. I think I'm dying. It's going to pound out of my chest and jump across the floor. My eyes fill with tears. I blink them away but they fill up again.

We didn't say anything to your mom, but we're going to. She doesn't deserve to have a lying daughter like you.

We're going to tell the whole class that you've been lying.

Where are you even?

Pick up the phone!

And then the last message. *We're heading over to your house now. Just so you know.*

The hand holding the phone is quivering. My legs are shaking. I almost can't even stand anymore. The last message was sent ten minutes ago! It takes fifteen minutes to walk from Olivia's house to Chaplin! I grab my shorts that are lying on the floor and hop into them. I tear off my sleep shirt and throw on my tank top from yesterday. I tug hard on the zipper of my shorts while I look for my shoes. Where are they?

Suddenly, Wilmer is standing in the room.

"Breakfast!" he says cheerfully, holding out two plates with bacon and eggs.

He's wearing the dumbest T-shirt ever. It's light blue and tight with a huge picture of Elsa and Anna from *Frozen* and the words SISTERS FOR LIFE written across the chest. He stands there smiling at me. I look at him for ten-hundredths of a second, but it's enough. Suddenly he's Wilmer, the old Wilmer. The one with the crooked front tooth and zero social antennae. The one who says outright that his dad is broke and he can't go on vacation. The one from the classroom and Olivia's party. The crazy neighbor who throws pebbles at the windows of people he doesn't even know. It *cannot* be true that I slept over with him, that I kissed him, that we've been playing in here for weeks like two little kids. Because now Olivia and Emma are on their way! And there could be nothing worse than being exposed by them.

"I can't play with you anymore!" I shout at Wilmer, holding out my phone. "Don't you understand how stupid this is? Playing like this? It's so unbelievably childish."

Wilmer's eyes go dark.

"You have to leave! *NOW*! The game is over. It's over!" I scream at him.

And then I run toward the door, fling it open, and take the steps two at a time up into the backyard. It's raining. I run past the sandbox and the clotheslines and the little patch of grass. My mouth tastes like blood. I can't see anyone standing outside Building A. I turn and run toward the entryway and stop under the sign that welcomes you to Craplin Court. I take out my phone and call Olivia, but she doesn't pick up. I send a text instead.

Don't go to my mom. I'll explain everything.

I can see them coming down the street about three minutes after the message is sent. The taste of blood is gone. I can breathe again. I hope it doesn't look like I've been crying. I try to smile to myself in the entryway, try to come up with a plan. But here they come. Olivia and Emma. With firm, determined steps. They come into the entryway, stop, and look at the sign for Craplin Court. Then they look over at me, glaring angrily. I'm a prisoner who's confessed, and they're out to get me.

"Hi," I say, attempting a smile. "Have you had a nice summer?"

They don't answer.

"You're in deep crap, Nora," Olivia says. "Why do you lie so much, really?"

I look at her. I don't know the answer. Or, I know the answer but can't say it. I feel small enough as it is. I don't need to get any smaller.

"We were walking past here and saw that the windows in your apartment were open, so I decided to come get my gift. We asked your mom if you'd had fun in the trop-ics, and she said you'd just been at home all summer."

"So then we sent that message last night, asking if you were having fun in the tropics, just to see what you'd an-swered," says Emma. "And you kept lying!"

She's out of breath.

"You lied to the whole class," she continues, exasperat-ed. "The pictures you posted were *fake*."

"And your mom thinks you're with some girl named Maria!" says Olivia.

They look at me like two policemen during an interro-gation. Why are they getting so involved with this?

"People who lie to your face are just super insulting," Emma says sharply, as if she knows what I was just thinking.

"Where have you *really* been?"

The taste of blood is back.

"Tell us the truth!"

I cross my fingers behind my back even though I know that doesn't help. Nothing will help at this point.

"I've kind of been in the tropics, in a way," I mumble, regretting it as soon as I say it.

"Seriously?!" Olivia and Emma chorus.

There is no solution. They're going to win anyway.

"It was Wilmer," I hear myself say. "The new guy in our class."

I point at Building F.

"He lives there, and we started talking and he came up with an idea."

My voice is quiet. I don't say any more. They look at me, curious.

"What idea did he come up with?" Emma asks.

I don't respond.

"Hello?"

"He found the tropics," I mumble, and it's only now that I realize my socks are wet. I ran out without any shoes and my feet are cold.

"I just went along with it because I didn't have anything else to do."

My voice gets a bit louder now.

"He found an empty caretaker's apartment," I say, realizing I need to tell them everything. "And then he made a kind of . . . tropics there. With a pool and stuff."

They look at me, their eyes wide.

"A pool?"

"Yeah, he's really weird," I say, seeing they're smiling now, like their suspicions are being confirmed.

"Like super childish, I guess."

Olivia and Emma look at each other.

"He pretends he's in the tropics. Down there," I say, pointing.

"Show us," Olivia says, starting to walk. "Otherwise we'll tell everyone you've been lying about the tropics."

e walk past the playset and the sandbox and the little patch of grass. A man is talking to himself over by the clotheslines, holding his hands up in front of his face and yelling at nothing.

"I've never been in here," Emma whispers. "But it's like really lame."

"It *is* called Craplin," Olivia says. "And I mean the name *fits*."

My socks make slapping sounds against the wet asphalt. I'm freezing in my tank top and thin shorts. There's a pressure behind my eyes, and I bite my lower lip. I absolutely cannot start crying now.

We're at the end of the backyard.

"There," I say, pointing at the stairs. "It's down there."

Olivia and Emma walk side by side down the stairs like they have to protect themselves from the dangers that might be waiting inside the basement door.

I think about Wilmer, who has no idea what's happening. Wilmer, who made bacon and eggs. My skin stings and I bite my lower lip again. All of a sudden I'm the old Nora again. Uncertain and afraid.

They look at the welcome sign.

"Who are Frida and Anton?" Olivia laughs.

I don't respond. They're just going to think it's lame. Stories about old caretakers with broken hearts.

The door is locked, but Wilmer taught me how to open it. You just have to flip up the lock with a coin or something hard. I have a quarter in my pocket and turn it in the lock until it clicks. I let them in. Into the tropics. Which is empty and quiet. The smell of bacon is strong. I'm hungry.

"Hello?" I call out.

No one answers. Wilmer must have done what I asked—gone home. Luckily, he isn't standing here in his lame T-shirt when Olivia and Emma arrive.

They stand there gawking by the red couch. They look around, pointing. Giggling. Whispering. Everything that is secret is revealed.

"What *is* this place? What's the deal?"

They look at the pink kiddie pool with the Hello Kitty pattern. At the sand on the floor, at the beach chair and towels. At my bathing suit and Wilmer's swim trunks hanging up to dry. They look at the sunset and the lights. The red parasol. They look at the sign: TRANQUIL TIMES SPA—WHERE DREAMS COME TRUE.

"Oh my God, this is so lame."

Suddenly I'm the old Nora again. Seeing things through new eyes. The same eyes as Olivia and Emma. It looks so lame. Everything. This entire stupid place we've made. I mean, the tropics, come on! I've known that this was childish and lame the whole time, even though it's been fun, too. The umbrella drinks from yesterday are still on the table. Yesterday seems like a hundred years ago. It's completely silent in here.

"Is this where you took the picture?" Olivia asks.

I nod. I can feel the tears. They can't come now. I can cry afterward.

"Wilmer's the one who did it," I say, feeling the tears disappearing.

My muscles tense up in a new way. I feel stronger. I have someone to hide behind, a kind of shield. I point at the pool and the umbrella drinks, at the beach chair and the parasol and the ugly wallpaper.

"He found it all on Craigslist," I say and laugh. It helps to laugh.

I roll my eyes. After all, it *was* Wilmer's idea to begin with. *He* was the one who wanted to make the tropics in the old caretaker's apartment. *He* was the one who broke in and started hanging out here.

"I've just been here once in a while," I lie.

"He seems like a total nerd," Emma says, and I nod.

"He *is* a total nerd," I say to confirm.

Now it's suddenly us against Wilmer. He doesn't fit in, and I really did know that already.

"He's kind of a . . . vacation friend," I continue, because this is going better than I'd thought it would. "Someone you're just friends with during vacation since you don't have anyone else to hang out with."

It looks like they get what I mean. They've probably had a lot of vacation friends, too, since they've traveled so much. And this is what I've been thinking anyway—that Wilmer is just someone I'm hanging out with now during summer break. I wasn't planning on being friends with him when school starts again and everyone can see us.

"And I think he really doesn't have the best situation at home," I say. "Since he's here like literally all the time."

They look at me, curious. It looks like they want more. More about Wilmer. *He's* the one they want to know about, not me and everything I've lied about.

"Tell us, then," Emma says eagerly.

"I think his dad drinks a lot," I say, thinking about what Wilmer told me about his only tropical vacation. "And his mom left them and had kids with a guy in Sweden. So he really only talks to her on FaceTime."

I see the looks on their faces. They want more. Even more. They're greedy.

"He's poor," I say. "He gets his clothes from his dad. Ugly T-shirts and shorts that are way too big. And his phone is super crappy. It dies like every five minutes and the pictures totally suck."

They laugh, looking at me like I'm the greatest comedian of all time. I take a breath, filling myself up with air.

"And he's only been on vacation once in his whole life. In the tropics. And then his dad was drunk the whole time, so it wasn't exactly a dream vacation."

Now they're gawking at each other. Only one vacation *ever*. Over all the summer and spring and winter breaks. How is that even possible?

"Jesus," Olivia says. "What a loser."

"I know," I say.

And it stings.

It's quiet. My speech is over. The comic has left the stage. I'm scared all over again.

"I'm sorry I lied," I say, feeling like a dog that's been caught in the act of doing something it knows it shouldn't.

Pleading and wagging my tail. They could throw a stick and I'd run after it to fetch it for them.

Olivia and Emma look at each other like they're discussing with their eyes whether or not to forgive me.

"It's okay," Olivia says suddenly. "But you have to promise to tell the truth from now on."

I nod with my little dog head.

"To your mom, too."

I nod again. After all, I have been thinking about telling Mom the truth about the thing with Maria, but it's just never been the right time.

We're quiet for a moment. But then I hear it.

A noise that seems to come from the kitchen. I freeze. Olivia and Emma look at each other. Then they look at me. I can't breathe. It can't be possible. Because then my life is over.

I walk quickly across the floor toward Sunlight Taverna. The door is open, and I go into the kitchen. It's completely silent. Completely empty. The two plates with bacon and eggs are sitting untouched on the table. One of the chairs has been knocked over.

I hear some short breaths. And then I see it. He's sitting on the floor, in the corner between the wall and the filthy stove. Curled up in a ball, his arms around his knees, not looking up. The curls on his head are completely still. His ears are big and open, like shells.

He heard it. Everything. Everything I said. Every single word.

I sprint up the stairs and away from the tropics. Olivia and Emma follow me. I quickly rub my hand over my face like I'm trying to wipe away Wilmer and what I just saw.

"What was that?" Olivia asks. "That noise?"

Wilmer in the corner. His head with all the curls. The fact that he wouldn't even look at me.

"Nothing," I say, feeling my throat tighten. "Just a door slamming shut somewhere, I guess."

I walk quickly across the backyard. Olivia and Emma pant after me. I don't want them to see my face. It must be completely transformed now. The sight of Wilmer curled up in the corner, still as a soldier in battle. I can't think about him. It's too painful. His curls and his ears. I *can't* think about him!

The backyard is gray and wet. The man who was talking to himself has thankfully disappeared. There's garbage in the sandbox—a couple of empty bottles and a plastic bag. On the first floor of Building C, someone has hung a blanket in front of a window. I think about the gardens and bushes in Solvang Heights. The big houses and terraces and bright curtains. The garages and the moms who have it together.

"What's up?" Emma says, breathing heavily. "Are you *so* busy or what?"

We've gotten all the way to the door of Building A. Why aren't they going home? I pull the door open and walk into the hallway, and they follow me. I don't manage to say anything, I just start going up the stairs. My throat feels swollen. One word and I'll burst into tears. I notice Olivia and Emma looking at the wall with cracks in the brick, at the row of dented mailboxes. It smells like fried food. The ceiling lamp blinks like the world's lamest dance club. Someone threw a container of food on the stairs between the first and second floors, and pieces of kebab lie strewn across the floor. The neighbors on the second floor are arguing and shouting like they usually do. A man's voice bellows. Olivia and Emma jump. The third floor smells like cigarette smoke. There are some butts lying over by the window.

They just keep staring, like they're on a safari in the slums.

I stop outside my door. My heart pounds.

"We're coming in," Emma says firmly, and I open the door to the tiny hallway.

"Hi, Nora," Mom calls from the living room.

Is her voice cheerful or tired or angry? I know Mom's voice pretty well, but right now I can't read it the way I normally can. There's too much else distracting me. Wilmer hiding by the stove. Everything I said.

Mom shows up in the doorway to the living room in sweatpants, her greasy hair piled in a bun on top of her head. She fits in *perfectly* in Craplin Court.

"Oh," she says, loosening her hair. "You're having friends over?"

She nervously pats at her hair, trying to get it to lie flat against her head.

"Hi, again," she says to Emma and Olivia.

She smells so weird. Sour or something. Maybe it's the wine from last night.

"Well, did you have a nice time at Maria's, then?" she asks, looking at me.

It's completely silent in the hallway. Olivia squirms, one arm pushing against me like a signal. Emma clears her throat quietly.

I bite my lip. The lips that were kissing Wilmer yesterday. The lips that spilled out so many words, so many terrible things. And it isn't even over yet.

I look at my mom. Into her eyes. I see her questioning face. I can't help but imagine if she starts crying. I don't want that to happen.

"Go into the living room and sit down," I say, carefully nudging Mom, who won't stop looking at me.

Olivia and Emma follow Mom and me into the living room. They look around the apartment. Our apartment that's half the size of Olivia's living room. We don't have gray couches with enough room for a whole class. We have a worn-out couch with a blanket over the back, and Mom is sitting on it now, looking nervous in her sweatpants.

I take a breath.

"Maria doesn't exist."

My voice is hoarse and weak, like soon there won't be any words left inside me.

Mom laughs. A strange, short laugh that's quickly over. Then she looks at me.

"Nora?" she says seriously. "What are you talking about?"

"She doesn't exist," I repeat.

My voice gets even weaker. Soon I won't have any breath left, either.

"I made her up."

Mom's mouth drops open. She shrinks into the couch. It looks like a million thoughts are running through her head.

"But . . ." she says, and then shuts her mouth.

"It's important that the truth comes out," Emma says. "Nora's been lying about quite a lot."

Mom's eyes go gray and transparent. It hurts to look at her.

"But . . . Where have you been if you haven't been with Maria, then?" Mom whispers.

It sounds like she's about to cry. I watch her blinking, trying to keep herself together.

"In the tropics," I sob.

Because now I can't do it anymore. My throat is too tight, and a thousand gallons of tears are pouring out of my eyes.

"The tropics?" Mom says, dismayed.

There aren't any more words. Not right now. All I have are tears. For Wilmer. For Mom. For everything I've said and done and lied about.

"There's a boy who's starting in our class," I can hear Olivia saying. "He lives here in Chaplin. And he's kind of made his own tropics in an empty apartment in the basement. With lots of stuff he found on Craigslist. And he got Nora in on it."

Mom's face runs behind my tears. I blink and see she's gotten up from the couch. She's suddenly standing there like a giant in sweatpants right in front of us. Her face is tense.

"But is he nice?" she asks in a loud voice. "This boy. Is he nice?"

"Yes," I squeak. "His name is Wilmer. He's nice."

And my heart shrivels up in my chest.

Olivia and Emma are smiling when they go out into the hallway. They seem pleased with themselves. They've finally revealed a liar. They've finally gotten to the bottom of it. The prisoner has confessed. The prisoner is sorry and feels bad, so they can walk out the door victorious.

Mom sits back down on the couch. She put her hair back up and her eyes are normal again. I've promised to show her the tropics later. Everything that's secret will be revealed. And I won't lie anymore. I said that with a clear voice so both Emma and Olivia heard it. From now on, only the truth. No matter what.

"One thing before we leave," says Olivia. "My birthday present. Do you have it, or what?"

I shake my head.

"That doesn't exist either," I say.

I'm so exposed now that it doesn't matter what other truths I tell her.

"I didn't have any money, and I didn't want to ask Mom since she gets so stressed out about birthdays and things that cost money. So I just pretended that I bought a present for you."

Olivia looks appalled. Like this is the most shocking thing that's been revealed today. Tears well up in her eyes.

Maybe she's never experienced anything worse than this.

Emma puts her arm protectively around her.

"Now I've told you everything," I say.

I shut the door and am empty.

Mom and I talk for a long time. I tell her things that until now I've only said to one person in the entire world. That I don't have any friends. That I don't want to ask for money even though I need it because I don't want her to get sad. That everyone else has expensive clothes and things and can buy presents for birthdays, that they all go on vacation abroad. That they live in nice houses in Solvang Heights while I live here, in Craplin, in an apartment that's smaller than the living rooms of most people in my class. That the others don't think about money at all because they always have money. And that I think about it almost all the time.

"Who have you talked to about this besides me?" Mom asks, and then I start sobbing again.

Because it's impossible to say the name without thinking about how he looked curled up in the corner of the kitchen. Without thinking about everything he heard.

Mom follows me to the tropics that afternoon.

My heart is pounding outside of my skin. Just a few feet left to go. I don't have any plan for what I'll say if Wilmer is sitting on the couch. There aren't any words in the whole world that can fix what's happened. I can't look him in the eye. I'm the absolute *worst* person in the whole universe. I broke a secret pact. In the most horrible way possible.

There's something at the top of the stairwell. Something pink. It takes a few seconds before I realize what it is. The Hello Kitty pool. One side has collapsed, and a puddle of rainwater has gathered in the corner.

We walk down the stairs. My stomach hurts when I see it. The sign is torn in two. FRIDA on one piece and ANTON on another, flung on the steps. Pieces of tape and a little bit of the pizza box are still stuck to the door.

"What is this place?" Mom whispers.

I fish out the quarter that's still in my shorts, stick it in the lock, and put my weight against the door. It opens with a click.

Mom walks in uncertainly, like I'm luring her into a trap where scary people might show up at any moment.

I turn on the harsh ceiling light, and the tropics come into view. But it isn't Wilmer's and my tropics anymore. It's a completely different place entirely.

The parasol is upturned. Mom's beach chair is folded

up and lying on the floor by Anton's desk. The sandy beach is spread out across the floor. The string of lights is thrown into a corner, the nails sticking out of the wall like barbed wire. The picture of Frida is gone. The book of poems and the envelope with the unsent letter are on the floor by the couch. The sunset has been torn apart, right where the pretty sun meets the palm trees.

I go into Sunlight Taverna. The mug from the Lillehammer Olympics lies in pieces on the floor. I look in the corner by the stove, just to be sure that he isn't still curled up there. The empty space makes me so sad.

All of the beauty products are in the sink in Tranquil Times Spa. Wilmer's beach towel is lying on the toilet.

Mom is still standing in the same spot out in the living room. It looks like she might start crying at any second. I thought she might understand a bit more if I took her here, but now with the way the place looks, it's a bit difficult to sell.

"Am I the worst mother in the world?" she whispers, looking at me.

I don't answer. I don't understand why this suddenly has to be about her.

"It's like I've been asleep," she continues. "And suddenly it's morning again."

"You have been tired for a pretty long time," I say carefully.

Mom nods.

"I just don't understand," she says, looking around. "Why have you been *here* all summer? I was so sure you were at the beach having fun. With Maria."

I don't say anything. I just go over to her and put my arms around her. I can hear her heart beating against my ear. I lean against her for a long time.

And then I see the ring. It's sitting on the desk. I walk over and put it on. I pick up the book of poems and the letter that had been lying on the floor and hold them against my chest. My heart feels like it's being torn apart. It's ruined. Everything that was good has been ruined.

I don't call Wilmer. I don't text him. I don't ring his doorbell. I don't go to the tropics.

His window is dark. His whole apartment is dark. I stand at the window in my room and look across the backyard, searching for signs that he still exists. That he wasn't just someone I made up, like Maria.

I can't stop thinking about what I'll say when I see him again. *If* I see him again. There are no words that are enough. No words that are right. I broke our pact. It isn't enough to just say sorry and assume that's okay. To say that I regret it. He'll probably never talk to me again.

The days pass.

I think about him about every three seconds. I start counting again—the days and hours that are left of summer vacation. The world's best and worst summer vacation. Thirteen days become twelve and eleven and ten. I sit with my phone in my hand, looking at his number. Then I put it down.

I dream about him almost every night. He's walking along a road full of cars, walking and walking down the road until he becomes a speck and disappears. He's leaning toward me, laughing his nice laugh, his curls bouncing, and then we kiss. He's sitting on the red couch in the tropics, which has suddenly turned into a boat out on the open sea. He sails away, disappearing in the waves, his curls getting wet and sticking to his head.

I read Anton's book of poems, laughing at his bad rhymes and the hopeless poem about stew. It makes me cry, like it was Wilmer who wrote it. To me. That I'm Frida. One of the poems is called "Sorry." I copy it and hang it on the wall over my bed. It's the first and last thing I see every day.

Now that both Maria and the tropics are gone, I have to bike to Grandma's every day while Mom is at her class. It seems like Grandma is moderately pleased with this solution.

"Don't you want to be with your friends?" she asks.

She asks the same thing every single day, even though I answer the same thing every single day. It was so convenient with those friends, those people my own age.

"I don't have any friends, Grandma," I say. "You know that."

And Grandma squirms in her chair, looks at the TV,

and turns up the volume. Because she prefers when everything is normal.

Mom has started making breakfast. She lays out my clothes. She makes things for dinner, not just frozen pizza. She asks how I'm doing several times a day, whether I'm okay. Her eyes are clear and inquisitive. She seems less tired, doesn't talk about the class, and doesn't change into sweatpants as soon as she comes through the door.

Mom says it's like she's been sleeping and now she's awake. For me, it's the opposite. I've been awake, but now I'm sleeping. Everything passes by without my caring at all.

Mom's shrimp dream finally comes true: One day, she comes home with an enormous bag. She hums in the kitchen as she slices bread, takes out butter and mayonnaise, and puts the shrimp in a bowl. She even bought dill at the store. She chops it up delicately. The doorbell rings and Mom asks me to get it. My heart prickles. Imagine if . . .

Grandma is standing outside. She smiles and hugs me tightly. My heart falls.

"Nora, Nora," Grandma says, slipping into the narrow hallway. "Tonight, we feast on shrimp!"

I lie down on my bed and hear Mom and Grandma setting the table in the living room, speaking in low voices.

"Does she really not have any friends?" Grandma asks. "When I was her age, I was out and about all day. It isn't normal for a twelve-year-old not to have any friends."

Mom hushes her and says, "I'm trying to make something happen."

They smile cheerfully when I come into the living room. The shrimp are ready, and there's a white tablecloth and pink napkins. Soda in my glass, and white wine for Mom and Grandma.

"There's nothing like shrimp in the summer," Grandma says, helping herself greedily.

What is it with grown-ups and shrimp? I think, watching Mom and Grandma shelling for dear life. They scarf down enormous shrimp sandwiches, wiping the mayonnaise from their mouths. One tower after the other of shrimp shells. Is this normal? Are *they* normal? Who is it that decides what's normal and what isn't for twelve-year-olds? And what is it Mom is trying to make happen?

I could ask, but I don't have the energy. I let everything pass by. I eat two shrimp and go to bed.

I wake up the next day to a buzzing from my phone. The sun is beating against the window and it smells like coffee in the apartment. My heart starts hammering again, just like when the doorbell rang. What if it's Wilmer? My phone is lighting up on the nightstand. I see a text on the screen, a single sentence:

Want to come to the beach today?

It's from Olivia. I read the text several times, my phone heavy in my hand. What should I answer? Just a few weeks ago I would've been thrilled to get a text from Olivia, to be able to go with her, of all people, to the beach.

Maybe she's gotten over the thing with the present. Maybe they've talked and figured out that I'm actually pretty okay, that I can be part of the gang. For a moment I imagine the groups outside at school. The seventh-grade groups. The *most important* groups of all groups. And in the middle of the most important is Olivia herself. And maybe me, too. I need a group. I *know* that I need friends who pull me up, not down. I need friends, period.

I open the message and start writing. *Yes*, I write, then delete it. *When?* I write, then delete it. *Just the two of us?* I write, then delete it. *That sounds fun*, I write, but before I can press send, another message comes through.

We'll be there at 11.

My bathing suit is still in the tropics, so I have to wear a bikini that's a little too small for me. I don't really need to sunbathe *that* much, I think, opening the curtains. It's probably almost ninety degrees out.

Mom is eating at the kitchen table.

"I'm going to the beach," I say.

Mom looks at me.

"Relax," I say. "I'm not lying! I'm going with the girls who were here. Olivia and Emma," I explain.

I haven't even thought about Marcus, or whether he's coming, too. Or if anyone else is coming, and how many of them are usually at the beach. What they're wearing and talking about. Whether Olivia and Emma are going to tell everyone about my lying about vacation and Wilmer. I get scared again. I would really rather go to Grandma's. Mom smiles happily. She's wearing a red sundress and looks alert. And it makes me so happy when she smiles.

"Have a ton of fun, Nora," she says, and winks at me as she takes a sip of coffee.

They're sitting on the grass. Olivia has a white bikini, a tan, and big sunglasses. Emma's hair is in a messy bun and she's wearing a red bikini. There's a group of boys sitting nearby. I recognize some of them from the eighth-grade class. I see Emma whisper something to Olivia and they wave at me.

"Hi," they say together, looking at each other and each giving me a quick, careful hug.

It feels like I'm interrupting something, like they were doing something secret right before I came. Olivia moves over a bit to make room for me on the blanket they're sitting on.

It's weird to sit on the same blanket as Olivia and Emma at the beach. I notice how the eighth-grade boys look at me. They've probably never noticed me before, but now they're looking at me just because I'm sitting here.

"All good?" Emma asks. I nod, even though I promised not to lie anymore.

Emma looks at Olivia. They don't say anything, but smile. Olivia asks if I want a cinnamon roll. I say yes. We all scarf down cinnamon rolls before we lie down to sunbathe.

"Here comes Marcus," Emma says after a while.

I turn and see Marcus strolling over in white shorts and a dark-blue T-shirt. I keep waiting for my heart to jump out of my chest like it always does when Marcus is nearby.

"Hi, girls," Marcus says, smiling.

He flings his bag on the ground and sits down on the blanket, right next to me. He smells like he always does: sunscreen and fabric softener. His hair has grown out a bit and he's gotten very tan. One of his arms brushes against my thigh. But my heart is still.

Marcus lies down on the blanket pretty close to me. I almost can't believe that I'm part of this gang, that I'm lying on the same blanket as Marcus and the most popular girls in our class, that I'm part of something new. Shouldn't I be incredibly happy?

"Had fun in the tropics, then?"

Marcus looks at me and laughs. They all laugh.

"Yeah," I say.

Because I *have* promised to tell the truth.

"That's great," Marcus says, smiling at Olivia and Emma.

"We told Marcus everything," Emma says. "Hope that's okay."

"Have you seen any more of Wilmer, then?" Olivia asks.

I don't want to talk about Wilmer right now.

"No," I say shortly.

"He's probably still in 'the tropics,'" Marcus says, making air quotes. "I'm excited to hear him talk about his vacation when school starts again."

They laugh again. The sun disappears behind a wispy cloud.

"But, are you guys like . . . friends?" Olivia asks, sitting up. "It's kind of important for us to know. Did you like hanging out with him?"

It's pretty inconvenient that I'm supposed to be telling the truth now. But if I don't lie, I'm going to start crying. And if I start crying, they'll think I'm lame. And if they think I'm lame, I still won't have any group to join when school starts. At least not a group that's cool.

So I shake my head and make a face, so they'll get that the thing with Wilmer was just stupid and childish—without me having really said it. And then they smile. And we laugh. And Olivia looks at Emma.

"Because now we're kind of trying to be friends with you," she says. "But if we're going to start hanging out with you, we'd rather not have Wilmer be part of it, too."

I nod, biting my lower lip.

"Good," says Olivia. "Because we promised your mom that we'll be nice."

I look at her.

"My mom?" I ask, not really understanding.

"Yeah," says Emma. "All she wants is for you to have some friends who actually exist."

"She sent me a message and asked us to invite you here," Olivia explains.

She puts her sunglasses on top of her head. A little smile lurks at the corners of her mouth.

I'm trying to make something happen. Mom whispering to Grandma. Why did I ever think they'd come up with this themselves? That they *actually* wanted me to go to the beach with them?

"Tell us more about Wilmer, then," Marcus says. "He seems so lame."

All three of them look at me eagerly, just like when we were in the tropics, and Olivia and Emma kept pushing for more, and I broke the pact.

I look at Marcus sitting there with his mouth hanging open. I look at Olivia and Emma, at how they're smiling, squeezed together. And then I understand everything. Absolutely everything. Which friends pull you up and which ones drag you down.

"No," I say loudly.

Because that's the best word I can come up with. The only word.

And then I get up, pack my things in my bag, and leave.

bike home as fast as I can. I push up the hills and fly into the backyard. I toss my bike aside and loosen my helmet. And then I hear it.

"Fuglesang!"

There's a voice shouting at me.

"It was Fuglesang!"

I turn and see Greta Brattberg coming toward Building A.

"Her name was Fuglesang! I remember it now. It means *birdsong* in Norwegian."

She's waving her hands and comes all the way over and stops in front of me, breathless.

"I kept trying to remember what the pretty girl was named. Anton Berntzen's fiancée. Ever since you and that nice friend of yours were at my place talking about the old days."

I don't say anything. *That nice friend.* It feels like such a long time ago that it could've been the old days, too.

"And now I've finally remembered," says Greta

Brattberg, looking pleased. "Frida Fuglesang." She sings the name.

"I guess she was pretty famous in Paris. She got together with a movie star or something."

Greta Brattberg looks at me like she's waiting for me to say something.

"Your friend told me you found quite a few things down in Anton's apartment. Letters and poems and an old photograph," she says eagerly.

She leans toward me all of a sudden.

"And it shouldn't be so hard to find her," she says secretively, handing me a piece of paper. "She might even think it would be nice to get it back, even though it was a long time ago."

Her eyes are wide. What is she saying?

"At least, I would've liked to get a book of poems that was all about me."

Greta Brattberg starts ambling back toward Building H.

"You should take that nice boy with you!" she shouts from over by the clotheslines.

I unfold the piece of paper and read the short text. Under the name Frida Fuglesang are four words: "Solvang Heights Senior Center." That's a pretty long way from Paris!

It should've been me and Wilmer biking together. Wilmer first and me following. Cycling through the streets to sort out the old love story. Wilmer should've been wearing the engagement ring, and I should've had the letter and book of poems in a bag on my handlebars. It should've been the two of us.

But it's just me. I'm going to fix the love story alone. The old and the new.

I park my bike outside Solvang Heights Senior Center. Two men are sitting in wheelchairs puffing on cigarettes. They look at me sternly.

It smells like dinner in the hallway, something fried. My eyes scan the names. My heart pounds. "Frida Fuglesang" is written next to three numbers: 515.

The corridor is long and has light-green walls. The doors are lined up one after the other. I pass 501, 503, walking down the quiet hallway.

A woman in a blue uniform suddenly appears.

"Where are you going?" she asks firmly.

I don't answer. I just stand there. I think about Wilmer again. If only he were here. The woman in the uniform wrinkles her forehead. It says "Wendy" on the name tag over her breast.

"I'm visiting Frida Fuglesang," I mumble.

"Frida Fuglesang?" she repeats, and looks at me skeptically. "But she never gets visitors. And who are you, might I ask?"

"A friend," I stammer, looking toward the door to room 515.

"Is that so," says Wendy.

It probably seems strange that Frida Fuglesang would suddenly have a friend who's twelve years old. Especially if she never gets visitors.

"Actually, she's a friend of my grandma's," I add, smiling as sweetly as I can.

"And have you been here before?" Wendy asks, still wrinkling her forehead.

"Yes," I answer quickly.

Wendy still looks skeptical.

"She's in her room," she says crabbily. "She probably can't handle a very long visit."

Frida Fuglesang's room is stark white and quiet. There's a huge bed in the middle of the room with blankets and a pink quilt on top. Two gray armchairs are by the window.

The curtains are drawn and there aren't any pictures on the walls.

I stand there wondering where Frida Fuglesang could be. The door to the bathroom is open, but there isn't anyone on the toilet or in the shower.

Then I hear it—a cough. From the pink quilt. It isn't blankets under there, it's her, Frida Fuglesang herself. I hold my breath. What am I even *doing*? Coming into a complete stranger's room and finding an old woman in bed! To give her an old love letter and a book of poorly rhyming poems.

Frida Fuglesang slowly sits up in her bed. She has short dark hair and looks frail. Her eyes are big and brown in her narrow face, like a curious dog. It's strange to think that this woman was once a model in Paris, but it's definitely her. She has a mole on one cheek. I can see she resembles the old picture of herself.

"What on earth is the meaning of all this?" Frida Fuglesang says in a quiet, husky voice.

Wilmer and I should've been here together, but it's just me. I clear my throat.

"I'm looking for Frida Fuglesang," I say quietly.

She raises her eyebrows.

"Well, that's me," she says.

I nod and decide there's no need for small talk and I get straight to the point.

"I was wondering if you've heard of Anton Berntzen?" I ask.

"Anton Berntzen?" Frida says in surprise. "If I've *heard* of Anton Berntzen?"

"He was the caretaker at Chaplin Court a long time ago."

It doesn't look like Frida Fuglesang understands any of what I'm saying. Her mouth has dropped open. She sits there beneath her pink quilt gawking at me, her eyes big and round. Her hands are resting on top of the quilt. I notice she's not wearing any rings.

I hold out the envelope.

"We found a letter. Me and Wilmer. But it was never sent."

Frida's eyes grow even wider.

"So we thought maybe it was time you got it."

I hand her the letter. Frida Fuglesang opens it and starts to read. She closes her mouth. Her eyes scan the short text. Her lips draw up in an arch. She's smiling.

"Well, I'll be damned," she mumbles.

"So you *have* heard of Anton Berntzen?" I ask eagerly.

"Heard of?" Frida says, and looks at me. "I've been thinking about Anton Berntzen every day of my life."

We smile at each other. I miss Wilmer. A lot.

"He thought about you, too," I say, handing her the red book of poems.

Frida looks at me a bit uncertainly before she starts leafing carefully from page to page. She reads and smiles. Laughs. Dabs away tears.

"I had no idea Anton was such a good poet," she says after having read for a while.

She looks at me, her eyes wide and glistening.

"He compared me to a stew!" she says enthusiastically. A tear trickles from her left eye and runs down her cheek. "No one's done that before."

I smile happily. Anton's words have finally made it to his love.

"Where in the world did you find this book?" Frida asks, looking at me curiously.

Wilmer. I tell her about Wilmer. It's like I've known Frida for ages. Since the old days. I tell her about the caretaker's apartment Wilmer discovered. How it looked. About everything Anton left behind. That I lied to everyone about the tropics. And that the basement apartment became a tropical paradise.

She looks thoughtful.

"Anton Berntzen wasn't good enough for me, in a way. After all, he was *only* a caretaker. That was what my parents used to say. They thought I could find someone better."

She sighs.

"And in the end I started believing it myself. I was so

easily influenced back then. I was so concerned with what everyone else thought that I forgot what I thought myself."

She looks at me.

"So when an offer came up in Paris, everyone said I had to go for it. They said I shouldn't throw away my life in a caretaker's apartment with Anton."

She smiles carefully.

"He was quite sad when I left," she says quietly. "He said he never wanted to see me again. He acted like he didn't care, so I didn't dare contact him. I felt like the worst person in the world."

She's quiet for a moment, her hand stroking the book.

"I couldn't possibly have known he was sitting in his apartment writing poems about me," she says. "If I'd known that, I would've come home right away."

Suddenly I remember the ring. Wilmer had been wearing it and now it's on mine. I have to pass it on.

"Maybe you want this back?"

Frida stares at me open-mouthed. She takes the ring, reading the text inside. "Your Anton. On the day of our engagement, August 16, 1962."

"Did you find his ring?" she asks. "It said 'Your Frida' on the inside. We put them on down in Anton's apartment."

"Maybe he never took it off," I say.

Frida smiles.

"Maybe," she says thoughtfully.

Frida looks at pictures of the tropics on my phone. She sighs and smiles. My heart feels like it's tearing in two. Me and Wilmer on the red couch, in front of the sunset, his arm around me, standing close together so we both get in the picture.

Suddenly the door opens, and Wendy sticks her head in.

"You must be tired now?" she asks, looking at Frida. It sounds like she's talking to a two-year-old. "Shall I ask the young lady to leave?"

Frida Fuglesang waves her hands in irritation.

"Absolutely not!" she says loudly. "This is the best visit I've had in a long time."

"You haven't had *any* visits in a long time," Wendy corrects.

"I'm aware of that," Frida says, annoyed. "But now I have a visitor."

She stares at Wendy.

"And you shouldn't discount that I'll be having even more visitors. What was he called again, your friend?"

"Wilmer," I say, and feel my face getting warm just from saying that nice name.

I can't look at Frida. I have to look down at the floor. My eyes are starting to prickle, and they're going to overflow if I look at her now.

Wendy shuts the door and it gets completely quiet. I can tell Frida is looking at me.

"There's something special about this boy, isn't there?" Frida says quietly.

I blink away the tears and hear her take a breath.

"Do you have a crush on him?"

"A crush?" I ask, looking up.

Frida looks at me. Seriously. There's something about her look. Even though I've never met her before, it's like she knows me. It's like she understands everything.

"Why isn't he with you today?" Frida asks, straightening up in her bed.

And it's the first time I've told all kinds of things to a total stranger. I tell her about Wilmer. How fun it is to be with him, how nice he looks in his lame T-shirts.

"He's so much more than just a vacation friend," I say, not even caring if I'm crying anymore.

I tell her about how he looked huddled in the corner by the stove and how he'd heard everything. All the terrible things I'd said and didn't mean. And that it's dark in his window now. From now on, everything is dark.

Frida hands me a handkerchief and looks at me for a long time.

"You have to make an apology," she says loudly.

"Make an apology," I say wearily. "That isn't something you say, is it?"

"No," says Frida Fuglesang. "But it should be. There's a big difference between *making* an apology and *apologizing*."

She smiles at me.

"My whole life, I've regretted not making an apology to Anton," she says. "Because maybe I hurt him so much that he could never really be happy again."

She suddenly takes my hand, and I can feel her ring against my palm.

"But you have the chance to make an apology. It isn't too late for you."

She squeezes my hand and smiles enthusiastically.

"And you have to seize that chance," she continues. "Take it from someone who knows what she's talking about. You *have* to make an apology, Nora. You have to hurry. Before it's too late."

It starts thundering as I'm biking back home. Loud, booming noises that seem to roll across the dark sky. Lightning crackles, and I only manage to count to one thousand and two before it thunders loudly. If only Wilmer were here, I wouldn't be so afraid. The red parasol, his hand over mine, his kind eyes. I think about Wilmer, Wilmer,

Wilmer all the way home. I say his name out loud to drown out the thunderclaps.

Make an apology. How do you *make* an apology?

There are eight days until school starts again. Eight days is the same as one hundred and ninety-two hours. I have eleven thousand five hundred and twenty minutes left.

make a list of ideas, just like when Wilmer and I built the tropics. I sit there for a long time wondering where I should begin, and then I come to a decision.

I jog through the backyard. I actually feel excited to get to the tropics, even though I know Wilmer won't be sitting on the red couch.

I pick open the lock. The room smells musty and everything is still a mess. He must not have been here since that terrible day.

I sweep the beach back together and go out into the backyard with a bucket to get more sand. The couple that's always arguing is standing by the sandbox. I sit down in it and fill the bucket. I can tell they're looking at me strangely, but I don't care. I just go right past them, back to the tropics. I scatter the sand across the beach, smiling.

I clean up Sunlight Taverna. I throw out the broken Olympics mug. I scrape the cold, greasy breakfasts off the plates and wash all the dishes. I throw out the empty pizza boxes. I shake out the tablecloth. I put a new candle in the candlestick.

I clean up Tranquil Times Spa. I empty the sink and put all of the things back in their place. I hang up Mom's white dress and shine the mirror. I unscrew the cap of the foot cream and sniff the pepperminty scent. I can hear Wilmer's voice in my head: *Relax, relax.*

I rinse out the Hello Kitty pool and tidy up the pool area. I put our beach towels and bathing suits back in their places. I fix up the pool bar with two clean glasses and put a pink umbrella in each of them.

The door sign is gone, but there's a pizza in the freezer in Sunlight Taverna. I take the pizza out of the box and put it back in the freezer. I find the scissors in Anton's toolbox. I think about Frida as I cut out a circle. Welcome to the Tropics, I write in big red letters, and hang it outside the door. I stand there for a long time, thinking. Wilmer and Nora's Paradise, I write underneath. It looks nice.

I find some tape in Anton's desk drawer. I start at the top of the wallpaper, taping the parts that were torn apart so the sunset is whole again. It takes some time to repair a sunset.

I hang the string of lights back on the nails. The same bulbs still work. Green, purple, blue, pink, and yellow. The light is back in the tropics. I sit down on the couch and look contentedly out over paradise.

I t's starting to get darker earlier. The August air is crisp and chilly. I stand outside the door to Building F for a long time, taking deep breaths as I lean back and look up at the window on the third floor. There's a faint light up there tonight. Maybe Wilmer is sitting in front of his computer. I cross my fingers behind my back and head toward the row of doorbells. "Wilmer and Tommy." The names are written in blue ballpoint pen. Capital letters, a little bit crooked. My finger rests on top of the button for a long time without pressing it. I clear my throat in case I need to talk into the intercom.

Then I press the button. Three hard jabs. I stand completely still and can feel every cell in my body battling each other. What am I going to say?

Nothing happens. I ring again. Four presses this time, short and light. I count inside me. *One thousand and one. One thousand and two.* Like I'm counting the seconds between a lightning bolt and thunder so I can tell how far away I am from the lightning. *One thousand and nine.* Nothing.

I walk out into the backyard. I look up at his window one last time.

And then I hear it.

"Hello?"

I run back to the door.

"Hello?"

It's his voice! It's Wilmer! I'm so happy to hear him that my throat tightens.

"Hi," I say, leaning toward the intercom. "It's Nora. Hi."

He doesn't answer. But I can hear his breathing.

"I just want to show you something, Wilmer."

Nothing. He hangs up.

My throat tightens even more. I go out into the backyard and look up at his window again. He's turned off the light. There's just a black square up there now. Maybe he's standing somewhere inside that square looking down at me. I lift my hand carefully in case he's looking out from all that darkness. I bend over and pick up some pebbles from the asphalt. I aim at his window and throw as hard as I can, but I can't reach it. I'm not as good at throwing as Wilmer is. The pebbles land on my head when they come back down. I try again. Again and again. But it's pointless.

His window is still dark, and I go home.

T here's a hundred and twenty hours until school starts. I put a letter in his mailbox. Wilmer and Tommy's mailbox. Wilmer's name is on the envelope.

I sat in my room writing all day yesterday. Probably a thousand words, maybe more. My fingers are sore after having filled so many pages only to crumple them up and throw them away.

The envelope lands in the mailbox with a dull thud. I have a thousand words to say to Wilmer, but there are only four words on the note. The most important. "I am so sorry."

There are four days until school starts.

Rain drums against the asphalt in the backyard. I'm standing in my room with my window open wide, the cold moist air giving me goose bumps. But I keep standing there anyway, looking over at Wilmer's window. Because there's a light on in there. I can see his head. All I have to do is wait.

And then . . .

His face. His curls. The crooked front tooth I can't see but that I know is behind his closed lips. He's standing in the window, still as a statue. I stand completely still as well. I can hear my heart. He looks at me. I look at him.

Then I raise my left hand, like a policeman directing traffic. Just like last time. But Wilmer doesn't move.

I reach for my phone on my nightstand, trying to look at Wilmer as I text. I press send.

I'm sorry.

He stands still for a few more seconds, but then I can see him reading the message. He looks up again, over at me. It looks like he's waiting for more. The pathetic little "I'm sorry" was far too little.

I'm the worst person in the world, I write. *I didn't mean to break our pact. Please. Forgive me.*

My messages shoot across the backyard like arrows, but they only meet a shield. Wilmer is still just standing there. I cross the fingers of my left hand. I wait and wait for my phone to buzz.

Wilmer stands there with his phone in his hand. It looks like he's typing. My stomach pounds, right beneath my heart. What could he be writing? It must be something more than just "okay" since it's taking so long.

Did you have a fight with the cool kids?

I stare at the little text for a long time. My phone buzzes again.

Need a "vacation friend" again?

Wilmer looks at me in the window. I'm standing completely still.

I don't care about them anymore, I write, looking at Wilmer. *I only care about you.*

I can see him reading. Then he disappears from the window. The light in his room goes out.

Two days until school starts. Mom comes home from her class and calls for me out in the hallway. She looks different. Her hair is shorter, her lips are red. She's wearing new white pants and big gold earrings.

"Put on something nice and come on," she says eagerly. "I'm not telling you where we're going."

There's a taxi waiting outside Craplin. Mom smiles secretively as we head to the other side of town.

"You can drop us off here," she says to the taxi driver and takes out her wallet.

We're standing outside a brightly lit restaurant.

"Now we're just going to have a nice time, Nora," Mom says, putting her hand on my back and pushing me into the restaurant.

We get a table by the window. Mom drinks wine and we each order three courses.

"There's something I need to tell you," Mom says.

She doesn't look tired. Her eyes are wide and alert.

Her mouth widens into a big smile. There's lipstick on one tooth.

"I got a job!"

She looks at me excitedly. I smile.

"In a flower shop," Mom says enthusiastically. "I've always been interested in plants and flowers."

I think about the dry, brown plants in the living room.

"So now things will be different for us," she continues, and raises her glass for a toast. "Maybe we can even go to the tropics."

She looks at me.

"To the real tropics, I mean."

"Blue Lagoon Deluxe?" I ask.

We laugh.

"Something like that," Mom says.

I ask Mom if I can borrow a little money.

"Of course," she says. "Is there something special you'll be using it for?"

I nod.

"I'm going to make an apology," I say. "To Wilmer."

Mom smiles with some chocolate mousse on the tip of her nose.

"Things work out for smart girls, Nora," she says. "Always remember that."

There are fifteen hours until school starts. I stand in front of the mirror looking at my new T-shirt. I went to a store that makes custom T-shirts. They looked at me a bit strangely when I ordered the text, but the shirt was done just a few hours later. I paid with the money from Mom.

My heart pounds behind the bright-yellow cotton. I look like a desperate Easter chicken who doesn't know what's good for it.

I bought almost forty dollars worth of things. Things I know Wilmer likes—soda and Cheetos and double pepperoni pizza. Everything is ready.

His window is dark and I get into bed. I lie there with my eyes wide open, thinking about tomorrow. The start of something new. Or the end.

Wilmer is wearing a red T-shirt in my dream that night. Red as a tropical sunset.

There are twelve minutes until school starts. The asphalt

in the playground is hot. The flag is raised. The groups are in place. Olivia and Emma are hanging out in front of the school. Marcus and some other boys are standing by the benches beneath the flagpole. It's almost like nothing has changed at all in the last fifty-four days.

There are three hundred and eighteen steps from the gym to the classroom. I walk right past Olivia and Emma in my yellow T-shirt. I can hear them laughing. I see Marcus staring at me. But I just keep walking, toward the entrance, up the stairs to the second floor, and into the new classroom, which is just your average classroom with a view of the playground.

I don't see him anywhere. Not in the playground. Not in here. The bell's going to ring in thirty seconds. Twenty. Ten. Now.

Ms. Gustavsen stands in front of us on the very first day of seventh grade. She's wearing a green skirt and floral blouse. Her hair hangs down over her shoulders, her lips glisten pink, and her nose is peeling.

"Welcome, my dears! Welcome to your first day as seventh graders," she says enthusiastically, throwing out her arms just like she always does.

It seems like she got to relax in her cabin in the woods; she doesn't seem to be able to stop talking and swaying around the classroom like an overjoyed hen.

"First of all," she says, going over to the cupboard to get something, "we'll see if your dreams for the summer came true."

She takes out the basket and hugs it against her breasts. Then, she starts bustling around to hand out the pieces of paper we wrote on the day before summer vacation started.

There's an empty desk by the door, two rows away

from me. Wilmer's desk. Imagine if he doesn't come. Imagine if he goes to a different school. Imagine if I can never make an apology.

My piece of paper lands on my desk. I unfold it and look at the three points, the things I thought would never happen.

"Go on vacation. Make a friend. Kiss."

"I promise not to ask you if it happened," Ms. Gustavsen says, and laughs so loudly it probably qualifies for a world record.

Then it happens. Finally. The door opens. He stands in the doorway looking anxiously into the classroom. His mouth is shut. His curls don't move at all. He doesn't say anything. He doesn't smile.

"There you are!" Ms. Gustavsen says, and walks toward the door to get Wilmer like he's two years old and needs to be led by an adult.

"Welcome!"

It feels like there's a thousand lightning strikes in my stomach. Wilmer! Both of my legs shake, and my heart and stomach and chest are pounding. My mouth is dry and my skin prickles.

He walks right past and sits at the empty desk. He doesn't look at me. He doesn't look at the T-shirt.

Ms. Gustavsen sucks the end of her glasses and looks

out over the class with her queen's gaze. And that's when I get things started. My plan. It happens now.

"Ms. Gustavsen! Ms. Gustavsen!" I shout, waving one arm. "Can we go around the class so everyone can talk about what they've done over the summer?"

A hissing sound spreads across the rows. Several people laugh. I'm pretty sure a lot of them know that the pictures I posted on Instagram were fake. Ms. Gustavsen looks a bit surprised.

"Well, sure. I guess we can talk a little about vacation first," she says a bit uncertainly, scrutinizing me with her gaze.

I stand up halfway and point at Vanessa, who's still sitting by the window in the first row, in order to organize everything in exactly the same way as before the summer. If I can just get this started now, it'll all happen naturally. Then I can follow my plan the way I've pictured it.

Vanessa had a great time in Italy, and Theo behind Vanessa had fun in Croatia. Simon experienced unbelievable things in Florida, and Alexandra thinks that Denmark is actually a dream vacation place even though she's looking forward to Thailand next year.

I look at Wilmer. His back is still. I can see the ears that heard all my terrible words. I straighten up in my chair and hear Olivia talk about how nice it was at the resort in Portugal. Emma rattles off everything she bought in Paris.

Soon it's my turn. Soon I have to tell. I'm ready.

Marcus talks about the south of France and Spain and Chelsea losing the match. It's boring. Uninteresting. I look at Wilmer while Marcus talks. His curls. I know how they smell, I think to myself, and smile while Julie spends forever comparing Cyprus with France.

Ms. Gustavsen takes off her glasses and looks at me.

"Now it's your turn, Nora," she says nervously.

Everyone turns. Absolutely everyone. Apart from Wilmer, who's still sitting completely still, staring down at his desk.

Someone snickers. A lot of people, actually. It seems like Olivia and Emma have told most people about my lies.

"This summer . . ." I start.

My voice is loud and clear. I straighten my back so everyone can see what's written on my T-shirt.

"This summer I went to the tropics."

A sound runs through the classroom, a gasp.

"Is this *actually* happening?" Olivia sputters, looking at Emma and Marcus.

"And it was the best vacation I've ever had," I continue, looking around the classroom.

"I did vacation things for weeks. With the world's best vacation friend."

Wilmer. His back in the white T-shirt. He turns

suddenly. His curls move on his head even though he's sitting completely still. His eyes are wide.

Emma suddenly flings her hand in the air and starts talking before Ms. Gustavsen has given her permission.

"Can't you just tell the *truth*? That you've been in Craplin Court all summer?"

She looks at me angrily. I'm happy I don't have to be on the student council and argue with her.

I stand up. It feels natural to stand.

"I *have* been in the tropics," I repeat calmly, looking at Emma like she's a little child I have to explain something complicated to.

"It's just a different kind of tropics from the one you're familiar with."

My voice is soft. My feet stand firmly on the ground.

"Because the tropics aren't a country," I explain. "You said that yourself."

Emma looks at Olivia. They gawk at each other.

"It's just a place you can go to relax and have fun, right? So then *I* can decide whether or not I've been in the tropics?"

I look at Wilmer. He's smiling! His mouth is half-open and his crooked front tooth looks good. He's staring at the text on my T-shirt.

WELCOME TO THE TROPICS.

WILMER AND NORA'S PARADISE.

It's the lamest T-shirt in the world, lamer than all of Wilmer's T-shirts put together. And I really do *not* look good in yellow.

"It was a dream summer," I say happily, waving my piece of paper. "Everything I wrote down actually happened."

I smile at Wilmer.

"I got a vacation friend for the rest of my life."

Wilmer looks at me. A big open-mouth smile. The kindest eyes. The lamest T-shirt, after mine.

"No, not just a vacation friend," I say. "A best friend. Or something like that."

I sit down calmly and notice that it's quiet.

No one snickers. For once, the classroom is quiet.

Well, what should we do now?" Wilmer asks when the first day of school is over and we're walking through the schoolyard.

I don't say anything, even though I know the answer. There's no question about it.

"First I want to show you something," I say. I take out my phone and pull up the photos.

"Guess who this is?"

I hand Wilmer my phone. He stops and stares at the screen. Then he looks up at me.

"You're kidding me!"

I smile at him and shake my head.

"It's Anton's girlfriend!" I say loudly.

"The pretty girl!" Wilmer whispers.

I nod and can't help my smile getting bigger.

The ring on Frida's finger, the book of poems she's holding in her hand. The mole on her cheek. I'm sitting next to her, holding out my arm to take a selfie. We're both smiling.

"Her name is Frida Fuglesang and she'd love to meet you!"

Wilmer looks at me, his mouth open.

"Frida Fuglesang," he says ceremoniously. "The tasty stew."

I laugh.

"She lives in Solvang Heights," I say. "And she's been thinking about Anton Berntzen every single day. Isn't that sad and wonderful at the same time?"

I take Wilmer's hand, holding it as we walk past all the groups. A lot of people turn to look at us. A lot of them laugh. Whether it's at the writing on my shirt or at us, it's all the same. I look straight ahead. Wilmer's hand fits perfectly in mine.

We walk out of the schoolyard toward Craplin Court. It's warm and muggy. Humid. Maybe a thunderstorm's coming, but it doesn't matter as long as we're walking side by side like we are now.

I got everything ready. The soda is in the fridge. The pizza is in the freezer. I made a playlist of new songs. I set the table for two in Sunlight Taverna. I put the beach chair under the red parasol. I hung up the sign with the same text as on my bright-yellow T-shirt that I just wore in front of the whole school.

I look at Wilmer. My wonderful vacation friend who's

maybe also a boyfriend. And then I finally answer his question. Because I know *exactly* what we're going to do now.

"We're going to have fun in the tropics, of course," I say.

And smile.